W9-BQJ-502

"Do you believe me now, Nikki?"

She glanced up and, like a magnet, her gaze automatically latched onto Jonas's mouth. Seeing the shape of his damp lips made her lick her own when she remembered why his was wet. Yes, she believed him. After the way he had devoured her mouth, she had no choice but to do so. And the thought that he had enjoyed the kiss as much as she had, sent her into a head spin. He was fire and if she thought she could play with him without getting burned, then she was only fooling herself. And her mother hadn't raised a fool. To keep her sanity, she needed to distance herself from him as

"You g— ... you can leave. In reality, he'd ... Hed snatched her common ... which was why she needed to hurry him out the door.

"Okay, I'll go, Nikki. But if you change your mind about coming on board for the Fulton project, let me know within the week."

She stared at him. Did he honestly think she could work with him now? Whenever she saw him, she wouldn't think of work; she would think of kisses.

Title Withdrawn

Books by Brenda Jackson

Kimani Romance

BRENDA JACKSON

is a die "heart" romantic who married her childhood sweetheart and still proudly wears the "going steady" ring he gave her when she was fifteen. Because she's always believed in the power of love, Brenda's stories always have happy endings. In her real-life love story, Brenda and her husband of thirty-nine years live in Jacksonville, Florida, and have two sons.

A *New York Times* and *USA TODAY* bestselling author of more than eighty-five romance titles, Brenda is a retiree from a major insurance company and now divides her time between family, writing and traveling with Gerald. You may write to Brenda at P.O. Box 28267, Jacksonville, Florida 32226; by email at AuthorBrendaJackson@gmail.com or visit her website, www.brendajackson.net.

NEW YORK TIMES AND USA TODAY BESTSELLING AUTHOR

BRENDA JACKSON

PRIVATE ARRANGEMENTS

If you purchased this book without a cover you should be aware
that this book is stolen property. It was reported as "unsold and
destroyed" to the publisher, and neither the author nor the
publisher has received any payment for this "stripped book."

To the man who is my first, my last, my everything,
Gerald Jackson, Sr.

To my fellow author, Adrianne Byrd, the Queen of Plots.
Thanks for letting me borrow Quinton Hinton
and his Doll House for a spell.

You do not have because you do not ask.
—*James* 4:2

 KIMANI PRESS™

ISBN-13: 978-0-373-86244-3

Recycling programs
for this product may
not exist in your area.

PRIVATE ARRANGEMENTS

Copyright © 2012 by Brenda Streater Jackson

All rights reserved. The reproduction, transmission or utilization of this work
in whole or in part in any form by any electronic, mechanical or other means,
now known or hereafter invented, including xerography, photocopying and
recording, or in any information storage or retrieval system, is forbidden
without written permission. For permission please contact Kimani Press,
225 Duncan Mill Road, Toronto, Ontario M3B 3K9, Canada.

This is a work of fiction. Names, characters, places and incidents are
either the product of the author's imagination or are used fictitiously,
and any resemblance to actual persons, living or dead, business establishments,
events or locales is entirely coincidental.

® and TM are trademarks. Trademarks indicated with ® are registered in
the United States Patent and Trademark Office, the Canadian Trade Marks
Office and/or other countries.

www.kimanipress.com

Printed in U.S.A.

Dear Reader,

You have to love those "Bad News" Steeles!

When I introduced the Steeles with Chance's story six years ago in *Solid Soul*, little did I know that I would be writing beyond Donovan's story, *Intimate Seduction*. But the more I wrote about the Steeles, the more I knew I had to tell you about their cousins—those other Steeles who live in Phoenix. They are the ones known as the "Bad News Steeles."

There are six brothers. So far you've been introduced to Galen and Eli and how they succumbed to love. Now in *Private Arrangements*, you'll get to meet, up close and personal, another "Bad News Steele"—Jonas. Jonas is a man who thinks he has it all figured out. He loves being a notorious player and has no plans to change. But that love-them-and-leave-them attitude gets challenged when he finds that he can't resist my heroine, Nikki Cartwright. I think you will enjoy seeing how far Jonas will go to keep from falling in love.

And there's an added character you'll want to meet if you haven't done so already. His name is Quinton Hinton. Be sure to check out fellow author Adrianne Byrd's *Unforgettable* and *House of Kings* series to get to know Quinton, and look for Quinton's own story in 2012.

Thank you for making the Steeles a very special family, and I look forward to bringing you more books of endless love and red-hot passion.

Happy reading!

Brenda Jackson

Prologue

"So, Jonas, what do you think?" Nicole Cartwright asked as she handed the man standing in front of her desk another photograph she'd taken a few days before.

She watched as Jonas Steele studied the photograph and then his green eyes found hers. The smile that touched his lips made her heart pound like crazy in her chest. His company, Ideas of Steele, was on the upward move, getting a lot of attention, and she felt fortunate to be a freelance photographer working with him on this particular project.

"These are great, Nikki, and just the shots I wanted," he said, handing the stack of photographs back to her. "I'm glad you agreed to help me out on such short notice. Three weeks wasn't a lot of time," he added.

"Thanks, and like I told you, I work better under pressure."

He opened his mouth to say something, but at that moment his cell phone rang.

She inhaled deeply as he shifted his gaze from her to focus on his telephone call. She wondered why on earth she was drawn to him so much. She certainly wasn't his type. Just last Sunday his face was plastered across the gossip pages; his name was linked to some former fashion model. And the week before, the papers had connected him to some senator's daughter. It was obvious he much preferred the Barbie-doll type—sleek and sophisticated, without a strand of hair out of place.

She pushed an errant curl back from her face and thought that certainly wasn't her. And there definitely wasn't anything sleek and sophisticated about her. Jeesh. She couldn't recall the last time she'd worn a dress.

She tried not to listen but couldn't help overhearing his conversation. He was confirming a date for tonight. She tried to not let it bother her that the man she'd had a secret crush on for close to a year was making plans to spend his evening with someone else. Story of her life.

For the past twenty-seven years she had been living in a dreamworld and it was time for her to wake up and realize she'd been living a friggin' fantasy. As much as she wanted to believe otherwise, she didn't have a soul mate out there after all. There was no knight in shining armor who would come charging in and whisk her away to a place where the two of them would live happily ever after. It was time for her to accept that marriages like her parents' and grandparents' happened just once—maybe twice—in a lifetime. They weren't the norm.

And, she thought as she glanced over at Jonas, a leopard couldn't change his spots. So why had she fallen for a man who didn't know the meaning of an exclusive affair with a woman? She looked down at her computer keyboard, trying to ignore the pain that sliced through her chest.

"Oh yeah, now where were we, Nikki?"

She glanced up, tempted to say, *Nowhere.* Instead she said, "I believe you needed me to print out more photos."

"Yes, that's right," he said, smiling.

She wondered if his smile was for the photos or the phone call he'd just ended. Deciding it wasn't any of her business, she stood and crossed the room to the printer. Her office was small but efficient. The one huge window had a beautiful view of Camelback Mountain.

At that moment he took another call and she figured it was probably another woman. But when he let out a loud whoop, she glanced over at him and saw the huge smile on his face.

When he hung up the phone, he was smiling from ear to ear. "That was my secretary. Gilbert Young's assistant called. We got the Thompson account! They were impressed with those brochures we gave them last week and don't need to see any more!"

She clapped her hands while grinning, not able to contain her own excitement. "That's wonderful, Jonas."

"Wonderful? That's fantastic. Simply amazing. Do you know how many other marketing outfits wanted that account?" he asked, crossing the room to her.

Before she knew what he was about to do, he reached out and pulled her into his arms for a hug. "And I owe it all to you, Nikki."

It was meant to be just a hug. She didn't know what happened, but the next thing she knew Jonas Steele was lowering his head and slanting his mouth over hers in one hell of a kiss.

Chapter 1

Eighteen months later

Jonas Steele felt an argument coming on.

"I hear you, Mom, but I just don't feel what you're saying," he spoke into his iPhone.

His lips tightened to a frown as he alighted from the shiny black BMW two-seater Roadster and glanced around while sliding his aviator-style sunglasses into the pocket of his jacket. *Whoa! But I'd love to feel all over on those,* he quickly thought when his gaze landed on the legs of a woman who was getting out of her car. And they were definitely a gorgeous pair. Long, smooth and shapely.

"You and I need to do lunch to discuss this further, Jonas."

His attention was immediately pulled back to the

conversation with his mother. He rolled his eyes heavenward. "I'd love to, Mom. Anytime. Any place. You are my number-one girl. But certain topics are off-limits."

He glanced back to where he'd seen the pair of sexy legs just seconds earlier only to find the owner gone. *Crap!* Frustration seeped into his pores. He would have loved seeing the rest of her; certainly he would not have been disappointed.

His frown deepened when his mother said, "That's utter nonsense, Jonas. You can't restrict me from certain topics. I'm your mother."

He shook his head as he made his way across the parking lot. He loved his mother to death, but lately, talking to the beautiful Eden Steele, former international fashion model and the woman who had captured his father's heart close to forty years ago, was draining on his senses. "True. However, you leave me no choice. With Galen and Eli married off, now you want to give your remaining four single sons grief, but we won't let you."

"You won't?"

"No. Although I can't speak for the others, I can speak for myself, and like I've told you numerous times before, I intend to be a bachelor for life."

Her soft chuckle flitted across the phone. "You sound so confident about that. Do I need to remind you that Galen and Eli used to tell me the same thing? And quite often, I might add. Now look what happened to them. Both got married in the last year."

Jonas didn't want to look. In fact, he didn't want to spend a single moment analyzing what could have possibly made two intelligent, fun-loving, die-hard womanizers like his brothers Galen and Eli fall in love. Galen had gotten married ten months ago, and Eli had tied the knot on Christmas Day. Granted, Jonas would be the first to admit they had married gorgeous women, but still, look how many women they'd given up to be committed for the rest of their lives to just one. It made no sense. Bottom line, Galen and Eli were whipped and the sad thing about it was it didn't seem to bother them.

And he was sure his mother had heard by now that another bachelor friend of theirs by the name of York Ellis, who lived in New York, was taking the plunge this weekend in time for Valentine's Day. Again, Jonas was convinced that like Galen and Eli, York needed to have his head examined for giving up his bachelor status.

"You will be here for dinner Thursday night, right?"

Her words intruded on his thoughts. "Do I have a choice?"

"There are always choices, Jonas."

Just like there are always consequences, he thought, remembering what had happened to his brother Mercury when he'd decided to skip one of their mother's weekly Thursday-night dinners. Before Mercury could get out of bed the next morning, Eden Steele had arrived on his doorstep. She had informed her AWOL son that since he had missed such an important family function, she was duty-bound to spend the entire day with him. And then she had the nerve to invite the woman Mercury had spent the night with to tag along. Their mother had deliberately overlooked Mercury's bed-them-but-never-wed-them policy when it came to women.

Since then, none of Eden's sons had been brave

enough to miss a Thursday night chow-down. The last thing any of them needed was an unexpected drop-in from Mommy Dearest.

"I'll be there, Mom," he said, deciding he needed to get her off the phone.

"I'll hold you to that, and you're welcome to bring a lady friend."

He caught himself. He was about to tell her he didn't have lady friends, just bed partners. "Thanks, but no thanks. As usual I'll come alone."

Then an idea popped into his head. "Since Galen and Brittany will mark their one-year anniversary in a couple of months, you might consider convincing them that you need a grandbaby or two. Heck, they might hit the jackpot and luck out with triplets like Cheyenne," he said of his cousin living in Charlotte.

"Hmm, triplets. You might have something there," his mother said thoughtfully.

He hoped so. Then maybe she could turn her attention away from him, Tyson, Mercury and Gannon. His brothers would owe him big-time if he could get her to do that. He smiled, deciding to go for the gusto and said, "You might not want to scare them with the multiple-births idea though. Just push for the single birth for now. Come to think of it, I'd love to have a little niece or nephew, and I know you and Dad would make the best grandparents any child could possibly have."

He inwardly chuckled as he moved toward the revolving doors. He'd just laid it on rather thick and if word got back to Galen of the seed he'd planted inside their mother's head, his oldest brother just might kill him. But then drastic times called for drastic measures.

"Personally, I would prefer a niece," he added. "I can see her now, cute as a button dressed in lacey pink." In all actuality, he couldn't see a damn thing, but his mother didn't have to know that.

"Yes, I can see her as well," Eden replied in a voice filled with excitement. Apparently the idea was growing on her and fast.

Jonas breathed out a deep sigh of relief. "Good."

"But I'm envisioning her dressed in lacey lavender instead of pink."

Whatever. He glanced around hoping that he would run into the owner of the legs he'd spotted a while ago. Although he didn't have a clue how the woman looked, with legs like hers she shouldn't be hard to spot.

"Well, I'm at the hotel for my business meeting and—"

"Hotel? Business meeting? Really, Jonas, I think you can do better than that. I wasn't born yesterday."

He fought back a smile. It was pretty damn sad when your own mother didn't trust your motives. "What I should have said is that I'm meeting someone for dinner at Timothy's." He was well aware that Timothy's, the restaurant inside the five-star Royal Blue Hotel, was one of his parents' favorite places in Phoenix.

"Oh. Nice choice. Are you still celebrating?"

He smiled. "Kind of."

Had it been a week ago already since he'd gotten word that his company had been chosen to spearhead a marketing campaign of a lifetime? Over the years, his marketing group, Ideas of Steele, had made pretty decent profits, but with this new project there was no doubt in his mind that he was about to pull in the big bucks. Eighteen months ago the Thompson account had helped to get his company's name out there, and now the Fulton account would blast it off the charts.

"Well, don't celebrate too much tonight. I don't want you to get sick. You know you can't hold liquor well."

He breathed out a deep sigh. "Thanks for reminding me. Now, I really have to go."

"I'll see you Thursday night."

"Okay. Goodbye, Mom." He clicked off the phone, both amused and curious, wondering which one of his brothers she would be calling to harass next.

He felt confident that whoever her next victim was, his single brothers would be able to keep Eden out of their business. Like him, when it came to the women they were involved with, they didn't think any further ahead than the present.

He glanced around the luxurious, immense lobby of the Royal Blue Hotel, taking in the polished marble floors, high ceiling and rich mahogany crown moldings. He could remember the first time he'd come here as a boy of ten. It was to attend a fashion show raising money for charity, and his mother had been one of the models. On that day he'd realized Eden Steele might be just "Mom" at home, but to the rest of the world, she was Eden, a renowned international fashion model whose face graced the covers of such magazines as *Vogue*, *Cosmo* and *Elle*.

Jonas's gaze shifted to the massive windows on one side of the lobby to take in the panoramic view of crimson-hued mountaintops. It had reached a high of seventy today, a beautiful day in February, which accounted for the picturesque sunset he was now seeing.

He checked his watch and saw that he was a good ten minutes early. He could use that extra time to get a drink at the bar, but he knew his mother was right. His system had very low tolerance for alcohol, and too much of the stuff made him sick. So to play it safe he kept within his limits and would usually end up being the designated driver.

Deciding against the drink, he slid his hands into his pockets and crossed the lobby to the restaurant. There was another reason he wished he could take that drink. Nikki Cartwright. The thought of meeting with her had him feeling tense. For any woman to have a Steele feeling that way was unheard of. But he knew the reason.

The kiss they had shared a year and a half ago.

He'd kissed plenty of women, but none had ever left any lingering effects like the one he'd shared with Nikki. And none had managed to haunt him like a drug even after all this time. It had been an innocent kiss, one neither of them had meant to happen, one that had caught her off guard as much as it had him.

He could clearly recall that day in her office. He had been so excited when he'd heard he'd gotten the Thompson account that he had pulled her into his arms to hug her, and the next thing he knew they were locking mouths. And it had been a kiss that had nearly knocked him off his feet. It had made him feel emotions he hadn't known he was capable of feeling. And it had scared the shit out of him.

Jonas would be honest enough to admit he'd been attracted to her from the start and could vividly recall the day they'd met.

It had been raining all week and that particular day was the worst. She had burst into his office soaked to the skin with her blouse and jeans plastered to her in a way that should have been outlawed. He doubted he would ever forget how her jeans had hugged that tight and round bottom of hers.

He had rushed to get her a towel, but not before taking in everything about her, even the way her short curly hair had gotten plastered to her head. And he hadn't missed how her nipples had shown through her wet blouse, or what a curvy body she had.

She had looked a total mess, but at the same time he thought she'd also looked simply gorgeous. He'd also fallen over backward when he'd gazed into her eyes. They were so dark they almost appeared navy blue. And her lips...with their seductive curve had tempted him to taste them on more than one occasion.

His attraction had been stronger than anything he'd ever encountered, and during the three weeks they had worked together it hadn't diminished one iota. And the thought that any woman could have that kind of hold on him unsettled him immensely.

He hadn't understood why the attraction was so intense. And at the time he definitely hadn't wanted it and had done a good job of fighting it until that day. He doubted that she knew what he'd gone through those three weeks. Nikki Cartwright was a looker, no doubt about that. But then all the women he dated were. However, none had provoked the kind of strong reaction from him that she had with that kiss.

In all his thirty-three years, no woman had dared to invade his dreams or made him envision sexual positions he'd like trying out just with her. His taste in women often varied, but he usually was drawn to the slim and sleek. But it was just the opposite with Nikki. She had curves. The jeans she always wore showed off a perfectly proportioned body. A body that had been plastered against his while he'd drowned in the sweetness of her mouth.

The kiss had nearly knocked him to his knees, which was the reason, when he'd finally released her mouth, he had quickly left her office and intentionally put distance between them for eighteen months.

Then why was he now seeking out the very woman he had tried staying away from? The one whose single kiss had him longing for more.

Shivers ran down his spine, and for an instant, he thought about turning around and canceling the meeting. But there was no way he could do that. For this new marketing campaign he needed the best photographer in the business and as far as he was concerned, Nikki was it.

He would just have to steel his senses and hold his own against her. He had hoped with the passing of time his desire for her would lessen, but he found that wasn't the case. When he'd seen her on Christmas day at his brother's wedding, he had been drawn to her even more, which was why he'd left the reception early.

When Jonas reached the top step that led to the restaurant, he could feel lust beginning to stir his insides and anticipation invading his senses. It was happening again and it seemed he couldn't do anything about it. No woman was supposed to have this sort of effect on him. Not Jonas Steele. The master of one-night stands. The man who had a revolving door in his bedroom and who was enjoying the single life and didn't mind the reputation he and his brothers had acquired over the years.

He loved the opposite sex—all shapes, sizes and

styles. Race, creed or color didn't mean a damn thing to him, nor did religious affiliation.

He was the fourth-oldest of Drew Steele's sons. Drew had been run out of Charlotte while in his twenties when his reputation as a womanizer had gotten the best of him. Fathers were threatening him with shotguns, and mothers were keeping their daughters locked behind closed doors. Jonas had heard the stories from family members many times over.

Luckily, Drew had finally met the woman he'd wanted, fallen in love, gotten married and had kept his wife pregnant for seven straight years, which accounted for he and his brothers being born within a year of one another.

Jonas didn't know of a better-suited couple than his parents. Or a more loving one. But then, happily married or not, unfortunately, his father had passed his testosterone-driven genes on to his six sons.

He quickened his steps, thinking testosterone be damned, he was determined to stay in control. He was the womanizer the society tabloids pegged him to be and was making no apologies. He had a reputation and was proud of it and felt he was living a good life. And to top things off, last week he had been awarded the marketing deal of a lifetime and he didn't intend to screw things up.

When he entered the restaurant he glanced around and saw Nikki sitting at a table across the room. She smiled when she saw him and he felt his stomach do a somersault. And as if on cue, his pulse began hammering away and air felt as if it were slowly being sucked out of his lungs. *Holy hell.*

He drew in a deep breath and tried purging the deep,

unwanted attraction for her out of his system. He moved across the room toward her, thinking that no matter what, he was in full control. And this time he would make sure things stayed that way.

Nikki Cartwright watched the man approaching her table with a stroll that was so sexy it bordered on sinful. She tightened her grip on the glass of water while trying to downplay the sensations rolling around in her belly.

Her instinctive response to Jonas Steele was something she should have gotten out of her system by now. There was no reason why a warm rush of desire was invading her insides, almost making it difficult for her to breathe.

Then she quickly decided that yes, there was a reason. Walking toward her had to be one of the most gorgeous men she'd ever seen. Tall, powerfully built, with dark wavy hair flowing around his shoulders, he was pure masculine sex on two legs.

A quick glance around the room indicated she wasn't the only female who thought so. There was nothing quite like a group of women taking the time to appreciate a good-looking man, and Jonas was definitely a looker. Eye candy of the most scrumptious kind.

She'd known working with him on that brochure wouldn't be easy. After all, he and his brothers were the hottest bachelors in Phoenix. They weren't known as the "Bad News" Steeles for nothing, and their reputations for being die-hard players were legendary. There was a joke around town that a woman hadn't been bedded unless she'd been bedded by a Steele. From what Nikki had heard, their skills in the bedroom were off the charts.

The air seemed to shiver the closer he got with a stride that emitted the masculine power that all Steele men seemed to possess. Like his brothers, he had inherited his mother's green eyes. Smokey Robinson eyes, she called them, as they were the same color of those of the legendary R & B soul singer. And then there were the rest of his prominent features—medium brown skin, strong chiseled jaw and one luscious looking pair of lips.

She'd heard that of all the Steele brothers, Jonas was the one everyone considered a rebel. He wore his hair longer than the others and owned a Harley. She understood he had several colorful tattoos on certain parts of his body. She definitely knew about the ones on both shoulders since she'd seen him a couple of times wearing muscle shirts.

Nikki wished she could look right past all six feet three inches of him, see beyond the well-toned muscles beneath the designer business suit that symbolized the growing success of his marketing company.

And more than anything, she wished she could look at his lips and not remember the kiss they'd shared that day.

Had it been a year and half ago when they had last worked together? When she'd constantly fought to control her attraction to him? An attraction that definitely had been one-sided.

Still, he had kissed her that day—she hadn't imagined it. They'd both been caught off guard; however, when he should have ended it, he'd kept right on kissing her, even deepening the kiss. And of course, she'd let him. When he'd finally come to his senses and let her go, he had mumbled something about being late for an appointment and had hightailed it out the door without once looking back.

The memory of that day sent a warm rush of sensations flowing through her, and she sighed. The man was not husband material. He didn't even believe in having a steady girl. She'd heard about his one-and-done policy. It had come as a surprise, a real shocker, when two of those "Bad News" Steeles had fallen in love and gotten married. In fact, Jonas's older brother Galen had married her best friend Brittany.

That left four brothers still single and swearing up and down Bell Road that they'd never fall in love. And she had no reason not to believe them. And as if to make that point solid, she'd heard the four had stepped up their game and were chasing skirts more so than ever these days, especially Jonas.

To break eye contact she glanced around the room again and saw every single female eye was still on him. And then, as if of its own accord, her gaze returned to slide over him. She appreciated what she was seeing. *Oh, mercy.*

With the eye of a photographer, she thought Jonas's features were picture perfect. She tried not to be one of those women who judged a man on looks, but his looks were so sharp, so compelling, so pinch-a-sister-in-the-butt gorgeous, it took everything she had not to start drooling.

"Hello, Nikki. Thanks for agreeing to meet with me."

She jumped at the deep baritone of his voice, which sounded like Barry White reincarnated. She had been so deep into her "Jonas" thoughts that she hadn't been aware he'd gotten close.

"Sorry if I scared you just now," he said.

"You didn't," she replied simply, forcing a smile to her lips. "I'd gotten lost in a few thoughts, that's all."

"I see."

Pulling herself together, Nikki watched as his body slid easily in the chair across from her. Sensations stirred in her tummy again. Unknowingly, he was playing havoc with her senses. Deciding there was no reason for her senses to suffer any more abuse, she spoke up. "When you called you said that you wanted to discuss something with me. A business proposition." Like there could be any other reason for him calling and asking to meet with her. In a way she was surprised that he wanted to use her services again, considering how they'd parted eighteen months ago.

Nikki crossed her legs, hoping the action would tamp down the tingling vibrations she felt between them. The man emitted testosterone that was attacking her big-time.

"We'll talk business later," he said, smiling.

Later? She lifted her brow, a little surprised by his comment. If they didn't talk business then what else were they supposed to talk about? Surely, he didn't intend to bring up that kiss.

"We haven't worked together in months. How have you been?" he asked her.

She stared at him. Evidently he had forgotten they had just seen each other at his brother's wedding on Christmas day. If he'd really wanted to catch up on her life he could have inquired about her well-being then. Instead he'd been too busy checking out the single ladies, friends of the bride from Memphis. He had done the courteous thing and spoken to her, but that was about all. It was as if he'd been careful to avoid any lengthy contact with her.

"I've been doing well."

He nodded. "That's good. I saw Eli and Stacey's wedding photos. As usual you did a great job."

"Thank you."

He was about to say something, but paused when the waiter approached with menus. Seriously, why all the small talk? she wondered. Why did he feel the need to lay on that lethal Steele charm in such a high dosage? Sharing a table with him had her nerves on edge. There was that usual degree of desire she always felt whenever she was near him, making a rush of heat flow through her body. She shifted in her chair.

"And what about you, Jonas? What are you up to these days?" she asked, like she didn't know. Like she didn't read those society tabloids.

"I've been staying busy. Just got back from a business trip to South Africa a few weeks ago. Enjoyed the trip."

"That's good," she said, deciding to study the menu that had been handed to her. He did the same, and she couldn't help taking a peek over the top of hers to do a close-up study of him.

Why was he smiling so much?

As if he read the inquiry in her gaze, he looked up and said, "Last week I received a very important call from Wesley Fulton."

She nodded, very much aware of who Wesley Fulton was. Who wasn't? The man was a self-made billionaire who was building a global financial empire.

"And I have reason to celebrate."

His words cut through her thoughts. She could hear the excitement in his voice. "Do you?"

"Yes. You might have read in the papers that Fulton Enterprises expanded into the airline industry by introducing what they're calling a luxury airship."

She nodded. "Yes, I did hear something about that."

There was no way she couldn't have since it had dominated the media lately. Fulton had hired the best technological minds and engineers to build what everyone was saying was the largest airliner in the world. In fact she'd heard it was so large it made the Airbus A380 look small in comparison. She had seen photographs and it appeared to be an airplane and zeppelin rolled into one, with such amenities as individual sleeping quarters, a nightclub, a movie theater, a casino and a restaurant.

"Ideas of Steele was selected to head up marketing for this venture."

Now Nikki understood why he was in such a cheerful mood. That was certainly good news for his firm. To be selected by Fulton was a feather in any business owner's cap. "That's wonderful, Jonas. Congratulations."

"Thank you." He features turned serious when he met her gaze. "And the reason I wanted to meet with you, Nikki, is because I'll need a good photographer and I want you as part of my team."

Her chest tightened. To know he wanted to include her as part of his high-profile marketing project was almost overwhelming. Especially considering how their relationship had somehow crossed the line the last time they'd worked together. Being a part of something as significant as the project he was talking about could make her career. And it definitely needed a boost right now, especially financially. The economy had taken a toll on just about everybody and freelance photography assignments weren't coming in as steadily as before. Lately she'd had to resort to doing weddings, anniversary parties and private photo shoots.

"I don't know what to say, Jonas."

He chuckled. "Say you'll hear me out over dinner while I tell you about the project. Hopefully, I'll be able to convince you to come on board."

She drew in a deep breath. "Of course I want to hear about it," she said. But then a voice out of nowhere whispered, *Go ahead and hear him out, but you might also want to consider turning him down. Think about it. Will you be able to endure being around him constantly? How will you handle that intense and mind-boggling attraction that eradicated your common sense the last time? Do you honestly want to go through that sort of torture again?*

Nikki inwardly sighed, thinking that no, she really didn't. But she would be crazy to turn down his offer. She had bills to pay, a roof to keep over her head and a body that needed to be fed on occasion. But then, it was that body she wasn't sure about when certain parts of it were so attuned to him. He could charm the panties off a woman without blinking, and that's what bothered her more than anything. When it came to Jonas Steele she needed to keep her panties on. She had a weakness for him and it was quite obvious the kiss they'd shared that day in her office had meant more to her than it had to him.

His voice broke into her thoughts. "I hope my timing

isn't bad and you're not involved in a project that I can't pull you away from."

She thought about the job offer she had received a few days ago. It was election year, and one of the candidates wanted her as part of his team. Following around a politician as his personal photographer for six months was something she'd prefer not doing. But she didn't want to hang around Jonas and constantly drool, either.

She drew in a deep breath and said, "I do have a job offer that came in a few days ago, but I haven't accepted it yet."

"Oh, with whom?"

"Senator Waylon Joseph's election campaign."

He stared at her. "Whatever amount they've offered you as a salary, I'll double it."

She blinked, not believing what he'd just said. "You will?"

"Yes. My business has been doing well, but what Fulton is offering is a chance of a lifetime. It'll take us to a whole other level and I want the best people on board to work with. And I consider you as one of the best. Your photography speaks for itself."

She was definitely flattered. The Joseph campaign had offered her a decent salary and to think Jonas was willing to double it had thrown her in shock. She forced herself to regroup. She needed to weigh her options and think things through with a level head.

"I'll cover the strategy plan I've come up with over dinner. I think you'll like it."

There was no doubt in her mind that she would like it. When it came to marketing strategies, Jonas was brilliant. His company was successful because he was picky about those he did business with. In the world of marketing, a stellar reputation was everything. And unlike some CEOs, who liked to delegate duties and play golf whenever they could, Jonas was very much hands-on.

She knew what coming on board as his photographer meant in the early stages of any project. They would work closely together again, just like that time before—sometimes way into the wee hours of the nights and on weekends. He would come in Monday through Friday dressed in his designer business suits, and then on the weekends, he would wear his T-shirts and jeans and ride around on his Harley. It was as if he were two different men, yet both were sexy as sin.

She would drool during the day and have salacious dreams of him at night. It had gotten harder and harder not to react to him when he was around. Hard to keep her nipples from pressing against her blouse and to keep her panties from getting wet each and every time he opened his mouth to release that deep, sexy baritone voice of his.

He kept looking at her now and she knew he was waiting for her response, so she said, "All right, Jonas, I'm curious to hear your plan."

He smiled, winked and went back to studying his menu. Nikki drew in a deep breath as she turned her attention to her own. But she couldn't ignore the play of emotions that spread through her. As usual, he was having that sort of effect on her and there was nothing she could do about it but sit there and suffer through it.

She wished there was a way after hearing him out that she could just thank him for considering her for the project and then graciously turn him down. But whether she wanted to admit it or not, she wanted the job.

She needed the job.

But what she needed even more was the use of her common sense when it came to Jonas. And she wasn't sure that was possible.

Chapter 2

Being around Nikki was doing a number on him, Jonas thought, taking another sip of his wine. Wasn't it just a short while ago he'd given himself a pep talk, confident that he would be the one in control during this meeting? But that was before he'd had to sit across from her for the past half hour or so. More than once he had to bite down on his tongue to keep from telling her how good she looked or how sweet she smelled. And her hair, that riotous mass of curls that she tossed about, made her features even more attractive.

Crap. When would this intense attraction for her end? And why was he feeling as if he was about to come out of his skin? And to make matters worse, he had a hard-on that was about to burst his zipper. Why was the thought of doing intimate things to Nikki so much in the forefront of his mind? Why hadn't time away from her eradicated her from his thoughts? And why did he remember that kiss as if it were just yesterday?

He shifted in his seat again, feeling edgy. Horny. Lusty. Those were physical states he usually never found himself in. Never had a reason to. As a rule, he got laid whenever he wanted, which was usually all the time. But at the moment, he felt sexually deprived. Overheated.

Where was a Tootsie Pop when he needed one? Sucking on one of those usually took his mind off his problems. Eight years ago when he'd quit smoking, his brothers had given him a huge bag of the lollipops as a joke. They had told him to lick one every time he got the urge to smoke, and pretend he was licking a woman's breast instead. It worked.

Now if he wouldn't feel so friggin' hot…

If there was any way he could remove his shirt and just sit there bare-chested, he would. His attraction to Nikki was overpowering his senses and he didn't like it at all. No woman was supposed to have this sort of effect on him. But he knew no way to stop it. He took another drink and felt a bit queasy. Why was he drinking the stuff? He knew why, and the main reason was sitting across from him.

He glanced at Nikki again. She wasn't what he would consider drop-dead gorgeous, but her beauty seemed to emit some sort of hypnotic appeal. Her eyes were dark, her nose the perfect size and shape for her face, and her lips were sensually full…and tasty, he remembered. Combined, the features on her medium-brown face were arresting, striking and expressive. For him a total turn-on.

He just didn't know what there was about her that tempted him to clear the table and spread her out on it and take her for the entrée as well as for dessert. Then he would proceed to lick and lap a body he had yet to see or touch underneath those jeans and shirt she normally wore. But he had a feeling she was hiding a body that was ultra sexy. Her curves hinted as much. What color bra was she wearing? What color pantics? Bikini cut, hip huggers or thong? He had a thing for sexy underwear on a woman.

He shifted in his chair, thinking he needed a Tootsie Pop and bad.

He put down his wineglass to cut into his steak. But each and every time he would glance up and stare at her lips, he would remember that kiss. And the memories were filling his head with more foolish thoughts... as well as questions he didn't have any answers to.

One question that stood out in the forefront was that if he'd been so attracted to her when they'd first met, why hadn't he hit on her long before that kiss? It wouldn't have been the first time he'd broken his strictly business rule by making a professional relationship personal. Hell, he was one who believed in taking advantage of any opportunity, business or personal. Then why hadn't he placed her on his "to-do" list long before their kiss that day?

He knew the answer without thinking hard about it. From the first, there had been something about his desire for Nikki Cartwright that wasn't normal. He'd sensed it. Felt it. And it had scared him. He had never reacted so viscerally to a woman before. She had a seductive air about her that had come across as effortless as breathing, and he was sure it was something she wasn't even aware she possessed.

Thoughts of her had begun taking up too much of his time, and he couldn't shake them off like he did with other women. It was as if they occupied the deep recesses of his mind and intended to stay forever. And Jonas Steele didn't do forever with any woman.

And there was also the fact that around her his active imagination was worse than ever. Some were so downright erotic they had startled even him. That much desire made him feel vulnerable, and it was a vulnerability he could and would not tolerate.

Things had gotten worse after the kiss. He had started comparing every single kiss after that with hers, and so far none could compare. And then at night, he would wake up in a sweat, alone in his bed, after dreaming of making love to her in positions that were probably outlawed in the United States and their territories.

At one time he'd thought the best thing to do was just to work her out of his system by sleeping with her. He figured that one good night of sex ought to do the trick. But then there was this inner fear that an all-nighter might not do anything but make him want some more. Then he would start begging.

And the thought of a Steele begging was unheard of. Totally out of the question. A damn mortal sin. Definitely something that wouldn't be happening anytime soon. Never.

Then why was he freaking out about a kiss that happened eighteen months ago?

He figured one of the main reasons was that he had tasted something in that kiss he'd never tasted before—

the type of passion that could ultimately be his downfall, his final hold on the world that he wanted for himself. The only world he could live in. A world filled with women, women and more women. He refused to let his body's reaction to one particular woman end what he considered the good life.

He needed a Tootsie Pop.

"So what's your marketing strategy for this project, Jonas?"

Her voice was low and seductive. He knew it wasn't intentional. That's the way it was. He glanced over at her. Was she wearing makeup? He couldn't tell. She had what most women would call natural beauty. And this wasn't the first time he'd noticed just how long her eyelashes were. Most women wore the fake ones to get that length, but he knew hers were the real deal.

His fingers tightened around the glass, and he took another sip before saying, "Fulton wants me to capitalize on the fact there hasn't been an airship of this kind since the Hindenburg...while at the same time minimizing the similarities." He breathed in her scent again, liking it even more, and getting more and more aroused by it.

Nikki nodded. She understood the reason Mr. Fulton would want that. It had been decades since the luxury airship exploded while attempting to dock. Of the ninety-seven passengers and crew on board, thirty-five people had lost their lives. If Fulton had built a similar airship, the last thing he would want people to remember was the fate of the original one.

"That tragedy was seventy-five years ago," she said. "I'm surprised no one has attempted to build another luxury airship of that kind before now."

"People have long memories," he said, pushing his plate aside and leaning back in his chair since he'd finished his meal. "Fortunately, the ones who do remember are no longer around to tell the story of that fateful day in May 1937."

He paused a moment and then added, "I remember reading about it in school. I had a history teacher who ranked the Hindenburg explosion right up there with the sinking of the Titanic."

Nikki could believe that. Both had been major catastrophes. She had studied the Hindenburg in school as well, and was well aware that the disaster had effectively destroyed the public's confidence in any type of giant, passenger-carrying air transportation of its kind, abruptly ending the era of the airship. But at the time they didn't have the technological advances of today. She'd heard the airship that Fulton had built was in a class all by itself, definitely a breakthrough in the world of air travel.

"My ultimate plan is to rebuild people's confidence in this type of air travel." Jonas interrupted her thoughts. "After the Titanic, people were leery of cruise ships, but now they don't give a thought to what happened with the Titanic years ago. I want the same mindset in getting the public back interested in luxury air travel. Especially on the airship *Velocity*."

She arched her brows. *"Velocity?"*

"Yes, that's the name of Fulton's airship, and when you think of the meaning I believe it will fit."

He leaned back in his chair. *"Velocity* is being billed as the wave of the future in air travel, and is capable of moving at four times the speed of sound and uses biofuel made from seaweed with minimum emissions."

"Seaweed?"

He chuckled. "Yes. Amazing, isn't it? Fulton will bring a hypersonic zeppelin-design aircraft into the present age. It guarantees a smooth flight and will trim the time getting from one place to another by fifty percent. Ideas of Steele's job is to tie everything together and present a package the public would want to buy into. When the *Velocity* is ready for its first series of air voyages in April, we want a sold-out airship. Fulton's designers have created a beauty that will be unveiled at a red-carpeted launch party in a few weeks."

Jonas paused a moment when the waiter returned to clear their table and give them a dessert menu. Jonas looked over at her and said, "Fulton is well aware the only people who will be passengers on his supersonic airship are the well-to-do, since a ticket won't be cheap. My job is to pique everyone's interest, restore their confidence in the safety of hypersonic travel and make sure those who can afford a ticket buy one. I will emphasize all the *Velocity* has to offer as a fun and exciting party airship."

He paused a moment, then continued, "I'll need photographs for the brochures, website, all the social networks I'll be using, as well as the mass media. The launch party will be held in Las Vegas. Then the next day the *Velocity* will take a trial flight, leaving Los Angeles, traveling to China, Australia, Dubai and Paris on a fourteen-day excursion. That's four continents. Fulton has invited certain members of the media, and a few celebrities. You will need to be on board for that too, to take as many marketing photos as you can."

Jonas met her gaze. "As my photographer I'd like you to attend all events as well as travel with me. We'll want to highlight the airship to its full advantage, to give it the best exposure."

Nikki breathed in deeply in an attempt to downplay the racing of her heart at the thought of all the time they would spend together. Here he was, sitting across from her, all business. She drew in a deep breath. Evidently he had put the kiss they'd shared out of his mind and was not still dwelling on it like she was. Had she really thought he would?

Get real, girl. Do you honestly think that kiss had any sort of lasting effect on him like it had on you? You're talking about a man who's kissed countless women. In his book, one is probably just as good as another. No big deal. So why are you letting it be a big deal for you? If he can feel total indifference then why can't you?

She knew the answer to that without much thought. As much as she boasted about no longer believing in fairy tales of love and forever-after, and as much as she told herself that she could play with the big boys, she knew she could not compete with the likes of Jonas Steele. Nor did she want to.

She had deep apprehensions when it came to him and they were apprehensions she couldn't shake off. What if her attraction to him intensified? What if it moved to another level, one that could cause her heartbreak in the end? Could she handle being a Jonas Steele castoff?

"Um, this dessert menu looks delicious. What would you like?" he asked.

What would I like? Having him wasn't such a bad idea. Deep, dark chocolate. The kind of delectable sweetness that you could wrap around your tongue, feast on for hours and still hunger for more. She wondered about those tattoos she'd heard he had. Where were they? How did they look? How would they taste under her tongue?

Suddenly she felt breathless and her heart was thumping like crazy in her chest. She should feel outright ashamed at the path her thoughts were taking. She needed to get a grip.

She took another sip of wine thinking any time spent around Jonas would drive her over the edge. Already she was imagining things she shouldn't. Like how his lower lip would taste being sucked into her mouth. She shifted in her seat and forced the thoughts away. And he thought they could work closely together again. Boy, he was wrong.

At that moment, considering everything, she knew what her answer regarding his job offer would be. She would be giving up a golden opportunity, one any photographer would love to have. But she had to think about her sanity.

"Nikki?"

She met his gaze. "Yes?"

"Dessert?"

It was hard to keep her mind on anything but Jonas, and that wasn't good. "Yes, the apple pie sounds delicious, but the slice is huge. That's more than I can eat."

He closed his menu. "No problem. We can share it."

She swallowed deeply. He wanted to share a slice of pie with her? To him that might be no big deal, but to her that was the beginning of trouble. It was so sad that he didn't see anything wrong with it.

"Nikki?"

If she kept skipping out on their conversations he

would begin questioning her attention span. "Okay, we can share it," she said and regretted the words the moment they left her lips. Sharing a slice of pie seemed too personal, and this was a business meeting. Wasn't doing something like that considered unprofessional? Evidently he didn't think so.

The waiter returned to take their dessert order. After he left, Jonas said, "I need to be up front with you. If you do take the job it will require long workdays, but I don't see it as being as exhausting as the last project we worked on together."

In a way Nikki wished that it would be. Then she would be too tired to do anything but collapse in bed each night. Too tired to replay over in her mind every nuance of feelings she'd encountered around him. And too tired to remember that one darn kiss that he'd already forgotten.

Jonas made it through dinner—barely. His gut had tightened each and every time he'd glanced up to see her mouth work while chewing her food. He imagined that same mouth working on him.

And sharing that slice of apple pie with her hadn't helped matters. They'd had their own utensils, but more than once he had been tempted to feed her from his fork, hoping that she licked it so he could cop her taste again.

He'd meant what he said about doubling whatever salary Joseph's campaign was offering her. One thing she didn't know was that Jonas had kept up with her over the past few months. He knew no big accounts had been knocking on her door.

Like he'd told her more than once, she was the best

and could handle a camera like nobody's business. And from the way she was acting she probably didn't even remember that kiss. She hadn't even brought it up. In fact she was acting like it had never happened. He didn't know whether he should be relieved or insulted. He wasn't conceited, but to think one of his kisses hadn't left a lasting effect on any woman was pretty damn annoying.

His thoughts drifted to what he'd told her about the job and the time they would spend together. She'd nodded and asked a few questions. Otherwise, she'd mainly listened while he had explained the marketing strategy to her. It was something he knew she could handle.

He only hoped and prayed he could handle it as well. That he would be able to keep his libido in check and his hands to himself. He had a voracious sexual appetite, and considering the fact he was already strongly attracted to Nikki, that meant he had to do whatever was necessary to stay in control at all times.

Control suddenly took a backseat when he looked at her chest. He really liked the shape of her breasts, which were pressing against her blouse. The tips of her nipples seemed like little hardened buds, as if she was aroused. That couldn't be the case when she was sitting over there eating the last of her pie and not paying him any attention.

His stomach tightened when she finished it off by licking the fork. He again imagined all the things he'd like her to do with that tongue. And since he already knew how it tasted, he could feel sensations stirring in his gut.

Knowing he had to stop thinking such racy thoughts,

he cleared his throat. "So, now that you know what the project will entail, do you have an answer for me now or do you need to sleep on it?" *And how about sleeping with me in the process?* He had to tighten his lips to keep from adding such a suggestion.

Before she could respond, the waiter came again to remove the last of their dishes and to leave him with the check.

It was then that she said, "Thanks for your consideration of me for the job, and I appreciate the offer. But I won't be able to take it, Jonas."

He blinked. Had he heard her right? Had she just turned him down? Shocked, he fought to keep the frown off his face. No woman had ever turned him down for anything. Business or pleasure.

There was a long pause and he knew she was waiting for him to say something, so he did. "Uh, all right. Would you like to order another cup of coffee?"

Hell, what else was he going to say? Tell her that it wasn't all right?

"No, I'll pass on the coffee. One cup was plenty for me. And thanks for being understanding about me not taking the job," she said.

Was he being understanding? He doubted it but decided to let her think whatever she wanted. Shouldn't he at least ask her why she had refused his offer? He quickly figured it wouldn't matter. There was nothing left for him to do but to move to the number-two person on the list, George Keller. George was a good photographer but could get on his last nerve at times. The thought of spending two weeks with the man had his teeth grinding.

"Well, thanks for dinner. I need to leave now."

And now on top of everything else, she was running out on him. Automatically, he stood as well. "You're welcome. If not this time, then maybe we can work together again on another project in the future."

She shrugged. "Possibly."

Possibly? Was she for real? Just what was with this *possibly* crap? His lips curved into a forced smile. "I'm glad you're willing to keep your options open," he said, trying to keep the sarcasm from his voice.

At that moment she moved around the table getting ready to leave, and he felt a sucker punch deep in his gut. Nikki Cartwright was wearing something other than jeans. She had on a very short dress that showed all of her curves and legs he was seeing for the very first time. Long, gorgeous legs.

His gaze ran up and down her body and his breath caught in his throat when he realized that she was the same woman whose legs he'd seen in the parking lot earlier. Damn. Holy, hot damn.

Before he could stop himself, he looked up, met her gaze and said in an incredulous voice, "You're wearing a dress."

There was something about the look in Jonas's eyes that gave Nikki pause. Was that heated lust in the dark depths staring at her like she was a slice of strawberry cheesecake with a scoop of French vanilla ice cream on top? He had never looked at her like this before. Not even after the time they'd kissed. She was more than certain that she would have remembered if he had.

She was definitely confused. Did seeing her in a dress finally make him aware that she was a woman in a way that kiss hadn't? She would have worn a dress around him a long time ago if she'd known it would grab this much attention.

She drew in a deep breath, feeling sexy and seductive for the first time in years. "Yes, I usually wear jeans or slacks because they're more comfortable for the work I do. But I decided to wear a dress tonight since I'm going to spend some time upstairs."

He lifted his brow. "Upstairs?"

"Yes, at Mavericks. Tonight is jazz night."

Jonas nodded. Mavericks was an upscale nightclub on the thirty-fifth floor that had a rooftop bar and a wraparound terrace that provided a panoramic view of the mountains and Phoenix's skyline.

He stared at her and her outfit for a moment, wondering if perhaps she had a date. Of course if she did it was none of his business. But still, for some reason, he wanted to know.

"Sorry, I hope I didn't detain you unnecessarily. I wouldn't want you to be late for your date," he heard himself saying.

She smiled. "I don't have a date. I like jazz and thought I'd spend my evening doing something other than watching television."

He lifted a brow. "You aren't meeting anyone?"

She frowned. "No. I don't need someone to take me out if I want to enjoy good music."

He was well aware of that. However, a woman who was alone and looked like her would be inviting male attention whether she wanted it or not. There was no way he wouldn't hit on her if he saw her sitting alone. Men made plays for attractive women with only one thing in mind. It was the way of life. He of all people should know.

Imagining her sitting alone in a club while listening to jazz didn't sit well with him. He met her gaze. "I don't have anything else to do tonight and I love jazz as well. Mind if I join you?"

Chapter 3

Nikki struggled to retain an expressionless face as she walked into Mavericks with Jonas by her side. She was determined that nothing would make her come unglued, even the feel of his hand in the center of her back as he led her toward an empty table.

"I think this is a good spot," he said, pulling out her chair.

She had to hand it to him and his brothers when it came to manners. They were on top of their game, and she knew their mother could be thanked for that. Eden Steele had raised her sons to be gentlemen. Becoming notorious playboys was their own doing.

"There's a nice crowd here tonight."

She had noticed that as well. She had found out about the lounge's jazz night from a woman in her aerobics class this morning. Like she'd told Jonas, she enjoyed jazz, mainly because her parents were huge fans and she and her brother had grown up listening to it.

"Would you like anything to drink?" he asked when a waiter materialized at their table.

Remembering what he'd told her over dessert about having to limit his drinks, she smiled and said, "Just a glass of water with lemon."

Jonas gave her order to the waiter. "And I'll have the same."

He glanced toward the stage. The musicians were still setting things up. "Looks like we made it before the start of the show."

"Yes, it looks that way."

She had turned her head to look around the lounge, but Jonas got the distinct impression she'd done so to avoid eye contact with him. Did he make her uncomfortable? Nervous?

Then again, she could be avoiding his eyes because she was upset that he had invited himself to join her. The waiter returned with their waters and he watched as she took her lemon and gently squeezed it into the water before lifting the glass up to her lips and taking a sip. He sat there, transfixed and aroused, as he watched her part her lips.

She caught him staring, tilted her head and asked, "Is anything wrong?"

If only you knew, he thought when he shifted his gaze from her lips to her eyes. Her short, curly dark brown hair crowned her face like a cap and emphasized the darkness of her eyes and her high cheekbones.

Her question didn't give him pause. His brothers claimed he could BS his way out of any question so he said, "No, nothing is wrong. I was thinking about your lemon."

She lifted a brow. "My lemon?"

"Yes. Did you know there aren't any in India? They use lime instead. I was disappointed when I visited there a few years ago and couldn't get any lemonade."

She smiled grimly and he figured she was probably thinking, *Whatever*.

"So what's your favorite jazz group?" he asked her as he squeezed his own lemon into his water, still picking up on her nervousness.

She shrugged. "I basically love all of them, but I grew up on music by the Diz. My parents were huge Dizzy Gillespie fans. I also like Branford Marsalis."

He nodded and smiled. "Same here. My parents enjoy listening to jazz as well, and my brothers and I grew up on the music. But nothing dominated our house like the Motown Sound."

He chuckled and then added, "My parents are actually members of Motown Is Forever Association, which is a group of die-hard Motown fans who meet once a year to get their old-school, back-in-the-day groove on."

Selecting another lemon off the tray he squeezed it into his drink. She had gotten quiet on him again. The conversations at the tables around them were low and steady, which made the quietness at their table all the more noticeable. He took a sip of his water and wondered what the heck he was doing here. Why was he determined not to let their time together end at Mavericks just yet?

He knew the answer. It was simple. He needed to know why the kiss they'd shared had done him in.

* * *

By the time the first artist hit the stage, Nikki's brain cells were almost fried. She was certain Jonas was generating just that much heat. She could actually feel it all over her body, in some places more so than others, which was why she tightened her legs together.

What was his secret when it came to women? Not only did he have the looks but he also had the gift of gab. Although she had very little to say, it seemed he was determined to keep the conversation going. She had discovered there were no lemons in India, that Walt Disney's body had not been put in cryonic storage and he was convinced a bar of soap between the bedsheets prevented your legs from cramping. She figured if anyone would know about the latter it would be him, considering the amount of time he probably spent in bed with women.

She tried shifting her focus off Jonas and onto the performer. He was killing his saxophone, emitting sensuous sound waves that floated in the room. She recognized the piece and always thought she liked it better with the words, but the sax player was giving her thought. Without the words of undying love, the music still had a message of its own. And the message was stroking her senses, stirring across her skin and caressing certain parts of her body.

"I don't understand why you'd come here alone, Nikki."

She glanced over at Jonas and saw he had tilted his head while studying her as if she was a complex object of some sort. Was she that hard to figure out? Evidently he was a man who thought a woman wasn't complete without a man. She would be the first to admit she assumed a man and woman complemented each other, but only when they were on the same accord. When they wanted the same things in life and when there were no misunderstandings about their relationship.

"Why wouldn't I come here alone?" she asked.

"Why would you feel the need to?" he countered.

At that moment she felt that she could respond to his questions several different ways since he evidently didn't understand that some women preferred peace to drama, solitude to unnecessary commotion. But more importantly, a loving relationship to a purely sexual one.

She left his question hanging for a few moments before finally saying, "I don't date much by choice. At the moment I don't have time for the games men like to play."

He met her gaze, held it while he took a sip of his water. "So you're one of *those* women."

He'd said it like "those" women were a dying breed. Probably were if he had anything to do with it. Since she knew exactly what he meant, she said proudly, "Not really. I stopped believing in forever-after a while ago. I don't mind having a good time myself. But on my own time."

Nikki was convinced when he curved his lips into a challenging smile that her already wet panties got even more soaked. "Your own time? An interesting concept. One you'd toss to the wind with the right man," he said, as if he knew that for certain.

She knew his words were both a challenge and an invitation. He was one of those Steeles, those "Bad News" Steeles, so he would think that way. He was of the mind-set that everything would begin and end in the bedroom. And the end result would be hot, sweaty, sexually satisfied bodies.

Nikki noticed the sudden darkening of his eyes and flaring of his nostrils. If she didn't know better she would think that the pure animal male in him had picked up an arousing element in her scent. She'd heard some men had the ability to do that. Men who were acutely in tune with a woman.

And she wished Jonas wouldn't look at her the way he was doing now, like he could see more than normal people could with those green eyes of his. It was as if he could see right through her blouse, past her bra, directly to her nipples, which were responding to everything male about him. Certain things a woman couldn't evade, and her response to a gorgeous man was one of them, no matter how wickedly sinful the man was. And he was wickedly sinful. From the crown of his wavy hair to the soles of the Salvatore Ferragamo shoes he was wearing.

Thinking too much quiet time had passed between them, she decided to address what he'd said. "By the 'right man,' you're talking about a man like you, I presume."

That sinfully sexy smile widened. "And what kind of man am I, Nikki?"

Why did he have to say her name with such passion, such sensuality? And why was he intent on engaging in what she considered wasteful conversation? He knew the kind of man he was; he certainly didn't need her to spell it out for him. But if he wanted to hear it directly from her lips then...

"You're a man who loves women. Not just one or two, but plenty. You'll never settle down with just one, nor do you want to. Life is about women and sex, but mostly sex and more sex. You play safe. You play fair. But you play. And you will always play."

Jonas shrugged. Yes, that pretty much sized him up and he had no shame. There would never be a single woman to capture his heart like they'd done to Galen and Eli. There would never be a woman to make him feel anything other than a tightening in his groin. And that's what was so hard for his mother to understand and accept. But eventually she would. She had no choice.

Instead of responding to what Nikki had said, since her words really needed no response, he settled back in his chair to continue listening to the music. And to think some more about the woman sitting across from him. She might not want the hot sheets, sex and more sex, but something about being here with him was getting to her. He was a hunter and could pick up the scent of an aroused woman a mile off. And some part of his presence, and their conversation, had turned her on. He was certain of it.

He had no doubt she wanted to believe everything she'd said. Although she hadn't admitted such, he had a feeling that deep down she did believe in that non-sense about forever-after. He'd bet at one time she'd been wrapped up in the notion of a house with the white picket fence, babies and the words of undying love from a man's lips.

Who was the real Nikki Cartwright? his mind demanded to know. She'd peeled off a layer tonight by wearing a dress instead of jeans, and he liked what he saw. Who would have thought she had legs that looked like that? Legs that could probably wrap around a man real tight, grip him pretty damn good while they had nitty-gritty, between-the-sheets sex.

He took a sip of his water and appreciated how the cold liquid flowed down his throat to cool his insides. He knew the score with her and conceded he needed to leave her alone. Her turning down his job offer was probably a smart move. And to be quite honest, he really didn't have any reason to be sitting here with her, sharing her table, and listening to jazz.

He had tried not to notice her at Eli's wedding when she'd moved around the room snapping photographs. She had looked cute then…and busy. To keep his attention off her he had pretended interest in a couple of single women who'd flown in to attend. He'd eventually left the wedding reception with one of them.

And talk about leaving…Jonas knew he should go, tell her it was nice seeing her again and that he regretted they wouldn't be working together again and that he understood. His jaw tightened knowing that was one lie he could not tell because he did not understand it. Why was she walking away from an opportunity that could ultimately boost her career?

"That was beautiful," she said when the saxophonist ended the song. Like others, she stood to applaud, and Jonas's gaze automatically lowered to her legs. What a pretty-damn-stunning pair of legs they were. He had never considered himself the leg man in the family— everyone knew that was Eli. His favorite part of a woman's body usually was the middle. Specifically, what lay at the juncture of her legs. All the others parts— the legs, the breasts, the thighs, hips and backside— just whet his appetite. And as he continued to stare at Nikki's legs he could feel not only his appetite being whet but also himself becoming fully aroused in one hell of a way.

"Wasn't that just great?" she asked him, sitting back down.

"Totally tantalizing," was his response. He knew she was talking about the jazz instrumental that had just been played. He was talking about her legs and her curves in that short dress.

When the waiter came and refilled their water glasses and brought more lemons, he settled farther into his seat. He would stay, enjoy the rest of the show and at the same time enjoy the woman...at least enjoy the company of the woman. He'd learned his lesson with women who thought they could change their thinking that a wedding came before the bedding. Nikki might think she had it down pat, but deep down she would still look for wedding bells. There were really no sure converts when it came to that sort of thing. Just the pretenders.

He'd run into several of those in his lifetime. And the last thing he wanted to do was get mixed up with another. He glanced at his watch, thinking it was time to bring this evening to an end. But for some reason, he couldn't. At least, not yet.

Nikki ran her fingers through her hair as she walked beside Jonas to her car. It was close to midnight and he had hung with her longer than she'd thought he would. She had figured he would leave at some point during the evening but surprisingly, he hadn't. In fact he genuinely seemed to have enjoyed the music as much as she had.

But she wasn't fooled into thinking that he hadn't

been trying to size her up, figure her out. More than once during the course of the evening, she had glanced across the table in the semi-darkened room to find those green eyes leveled on her. It had been during those times, when her heart would beat like crazy in her chest, that she wished she had something stronger to drink than just water.

She was convinced there weren't too many men like Jonas Steele, then quickly remembered there were six of them, four still single. But each was different in his own way, although when it came to women there were definite similarities.

When he led her straight to her car, she glanced up at him. "How did you know this car was mine? I didn't tell you what I was driving, and it's different from the last one I had when we worked together before."

He smiled. "I knew it was yours was because I saw you when you got out of it, although I didn't know it was you at the time. I recognized the legs later."

She stared at him, saw he was dead serious and couldn't help but laugh.

"What's so funny? "

If he didn't know… "Nothing," she said, shaking her head. She pulled the key from her purse. "Well, I'll be seeing you."

"I'll follow you."

She lifted a brow. "Why?"

"To make sure you get home okay."

She looked at him like he had a visible dent in his brain. "You don't have to do that. It's not like we've been out on a date or anything."

"It doesn't matter. We've spent the evening together

and it's late. There's no way I'll not make sure you get home. I wasn't raised that way."

She let out an exaggerated breath. "What if I get your number and just text you to let you know that I made it home?"

"Unless you deleted it, you already have my number from the last time we worked together. But texting me won't work. I removed that feature from my phone."

"You did? Why?"

He shrugged. "I was getting too many unnecessary messages."

"Yeah, I bet." She brushed a curl back from her face. "Look, Jonas, your wanting to make sure I get home safe and sound is thoughtful but truly not necessary."

"Your opinion, not mine. Ready to go?"

When she saw there was no use standing in the middle of the hotel's parking lot arguing with him, she opened her car door to get in. She then watched in her rearview mirror as he crossed the lot to his car. As she turned on the ignition, she shook her head. He had recognized her legs. Of all things.

She pulled out of the parking lot and another glance in the rearview mirror showed he was right on her tail. *Right on her tail.* That same heat she'd been battling between her legs all evening returned at the thought. Okay, she was an intelligent and sensible woman, but that didn't mean she couldn't get tempted every once in a while. Just as long as she didn't ever yield to such temptation, she was safe.

Still in the mood for jazz, she turned on the CD player in her car and the sound of Miles Davis flowed through, bringing back the mood that had been set earlier. Good music and the presence of a handsome man sitting at her table. It hadn't been a date, she reminded herself, although it had appeared as such.

It took twenty minutes to get home and she tried not to think of the man following her. Every time she would look in her rearview mirror he seemed to be staring back right at her. And when she pulled into her driveway she was surprised when he pulled right in behind her. It would have been fine if he had parked on the street.

Her throat tightened when he joined her on the walkway. "You don't have to walk me to the door, Jonas."

His lips curved into a wide grin. "Yes, I do."

She eyed him, one brow arching. Did he have an ulterior motive for wanting to walk her to the door? Was he hoping she would invite him in? Did she want to?

She wondered what kind of game he was playing with her now, and more importantly, why she was letting him. She'd given him her answer regarding working with him again—a decision she figured she would regret in the morning.

In a way she was already regretting it. But her sanity and peace of mind were more important and she was certain working with him again would rob her of both.

"Your key, please."

She blinked when his request jerked her back to the here and now. She looked up at him. They were at her front door. "My key?"

"Yes."

"Why would you want my key?"

"To see you properly inside."

Yeah. Right. He wouldn't be the first man who tried testing her, and she knew he wouldn't be the last. But then she also knew that this was Jonas Steele, a man who'd probably perfected his game. And for some reason he intended to try his game on her. Did she have something plastered on her forehead that said, *Try me?*

"Thanks, but I don't need you to see me inside, properly or otherwise," she said, using the key to unlock the door herself. "This is where we part ways."

"Do you really want to do that?" he asked, easing closer to her, too close for her comfort. His cologne was getting to her. His very presence was getting to her.

"Why wouldn't I? Besides, we both know I'm not your type."

He chuckled. "And what is my type?"

She blew out a breath, feeling herself getting annoyed. "Someone who enjoys playing your kind of games." She'd thought that she would, had convinced herself she could handle a man like him if she began thinking like he did, but she saw that wasn't working.

He inched closer. "And you don't enjoy playing my sort of games, Nikki?"

That answer was easy. "No, I'll pass."

"You're really not going to invite me in?"

He actually looked crushed, but she knew it was a put-on, just one of the many faces of Jonas Steele. He played whichever one worked at the time. "No. Sorry. Usually a woman invites a man inside when she offers him coffee, tea or something else to drink. I'm plum out of everything. I didn't make it to the grocery store this week."

He leaned against her door front. "We do pretty good on just water."

"I don't have any lemons," she said quickly

"We'll find our own pucker power," he said, easing a little closer to her. He had taken off his suit jacket and tie and was standing there, under her porch light, looking laid-back, cool and calm. And it didn't help matters when his gaze roamed over her. He was up to something and she felt she deserved to know what.

"Okay, Jonas, what's going on?"

"What makes you think something is going on? And what kinds of games do you think I like playing?"

Another simple answer. "Musical beds, for starters."

He nodded slowly. Then a smile touched his lips. "Are you worried about your fair share of my time in the bedroom?"

The man was impossible. Now she saw she'd done the right thing in turning down his offer for that job. "I wouldn't have been the one who needed to worry," she said snappily and regretted her words the moment they'd left her lips. Of course he would see it as a challenge. The notion was written all over his face.

"Umm, that would be interesting."

"Not if you can't even remember a kiss," she muttered under her breath and then wished she hadn't when he stared at her, letting her know he'd heard her.

"Oh, I definitely remember it, Nikki."

She waved off his words. "Whatever."

"Um, maybe we need to go inside and talk about that kiss."

She shook her head. "No, we don't. We can say our good-nights right here."

"Not until we talk. Evidently we aren't on the same page."

"Doesn't matter to me," she lied.

"It does to me. It won't take more than five minutes to clear this up."

There really was nothing to clear up, but she figured

she would be wasting her time trying to convince him of that. Besides, deep down she was curious about what he had to say. Men could talk their way in or out of anything. But what concerned her now more than anything was why he was coming on to her after all this time.

"I'm going to ask you again, Jonas. What's going on? Why are you trying to do me?" A girl couldn't ask any plainer than that.

He inched even closer. "Because the thought of doing you has been on my mind ever since that kiss."

She stared at him. Did he honestly think she would believe that? There was no way he could convince her that that kiss had meant anything to him. It wasn't like they lived in separate towns and it wasn't as if she was hard to find. Her best friend was married to his oldest brother, for heaven's sake.

Besides, if a Steele wanted a woman he strategized things to his advantage and went after her with no time wasted. Eighteen months had gone by and he hadn't made a move. They had run into each other at several functions and he'd deliberately gone out of his way to avoid her. She wasn't stupid.

She must have worn the look of disbelief well because he then said, "You don't believe me."

She shook her head. "No, I don't believe you. Good night."

He stuck out his hand to block her entrance inside. "What about another kiss? One for the road."

Nikki drew in a deep breath because deep down, she wanted another kiss. No joke. All she had to do was look at his mouth and remember the taste of it. Good Lord, how could she think of such things and especially with this man? The man who had a player's card with no expiration date.

"What would another kiss do, Jonas?"

"Prove you wrong."

Could it? She doubted it. But...

She studied his features. There was a look in his eyes that was more intense than the way he'd been staring at her in Mavericks. She let out a frustrating sigh. That's another reason she thought she wasn't cut out to be in the fast lane. A woman could get gray hairs trying to figure a man out. "A kiss and then you'll go away?" she asked softly, feeling her resistance to him slipping away.

"Yes. Scout's honor."

She stared at him for a moment and then said, "I'm taking you at your word." She opened the door and moved inside with him following quickly on her heels as if he thought she would change her mind.

Jonas closed the door behind him as both desire and tension stirred deep in the pit of his stomach. He glanced around. She had left a light burning on a table in the foyer, and he figured chances were she wouldn't invite him in to see the rest of the house, which was fine with him. All he needed was the area where they were standing.

She was in front of him, looking agitated and annoyed, ready for him to kiss her and get it over with. His jaw twitched as irritation filled him. First she turned down his job offer, and now she was trying to rush him off like he was a bother. And she even had the gall to tap her foot.

She tilted her head back and looked up at him. "Well?"

"Well?" he countered, moving a little closer to her.

"What are you waiting for?" she asked, lifting her chin.

"For you to get your mind in check."

Sighing, Nikki doubted that would happen. Her mind would never be fully in check when it came to Jonas. She really didn't understand what the big deal was. Why was he taking so long to kiss her? He was the one who suggested they do it again. She would have been perfectly satisfied with her memories.

"You have beautiful eyes, Nikki."

She blinked and her heart began beating a little harder when she noticed he had eased even closer to her. When had he done that? "Thank you. You have beautiful eyes yourself."

His lips curved into a smile as he took a step closer. Instinctively, she took a step back. He reached out and gently grabbed her around the waist. "Where do you think you're going?"

"Nowhere."

He towered over her, but his face was close, almost right in hers. His breath smelled of lemons and she recalled what he'd said about pucker power. "Why are you taking so long?"

"Nikki," he said in what sounded like an exasperated tone. "Some things you can't rush. Be patient. Besides, I'm thinking about a few things."

She cocked a brow. "What things?"

"Like how much I enjoyed kissing you the last time. How your taste remained on my tongue for days, months, and how no degree of brushing could get it off."

She looked stunned. "That's impossible. You left, almost knocking over my trash can in your rush to leave."

He reached out and lifted her chin. "It was either that or I stripped off your clothes and took you right there where you stood."

He spoke the words low and all but breathed them against her lips, making her pulse quicken and her heart rate increase. "I don't believe you," she whispered as a shiver of desire ran all through her.

"Then maybe I need to make a believer out of you."

He advanced. Instinctively she backed up again until she noticed the wall at her spine. She also noticed something else. He had braced his hands on the walls on both sides of her head, caging her in. When he shifted positions the lower part of him rubbed against her middle. He was hard. Extremely hard. Diabolically hard.

"Why is your heart beating so fast, Nikki?" he asked, moving his lips even closer.

"It's not."

"Yes, it is. I hear it. I can feel it."

She swallowed, thinking he probably could. When she'd decided to go ahead with the kiss she'd figured it would be an even exchange. It was something they both wanted. But now she had a feeling she would be paying a bigger price than he would.

She stared into his gaze and he stared back, but there was something in his look that gave her pause, made her heart, which was already beating like crazy, thump even faster. And was the floor actually moving beneath her feet?

"Place your hands on my shoulders. Both of them."

His words were whispered across her lips, and automatically she lifted her arms to comply. The air between them was electrified, charged. She didn't just place her hands on his shoulders; instinctively her fingertips dug into his shoulder blades. If he was bothered by it, he didn't let on. Instead his gaze moved from her eyes to her mouth and she watched as he gave her a soft smile.

She focused her attention on the shape of his lips and wondered about their texture. Their taste. And then before she could take her next breath, his mouth lowered to hers.

Chapter 4

Jonas felt as if he'd come back to a place he should never have left. Never had kissing a woman made him feel that way before. The memories he had of their last kiss hadn't done it justice. His lips felt like a magnet, fused to her in the most intimate way. The heat that had blazed to life the moment his mouth touched hers had his body quivering inside.

He was taking her mouth with a hunger that he felt all the way down to the soles of his feet. This was no mere kiss. This wasn't even about reacquainting their mouths. This was the forging of fires in the broadest sense of the word. He didn't want just to play on her senses, he wanted to dominate them. His mouth was relentless, untiring and filled with a hunger that had him devouring her as his tongue mated fiercely with hers.

A man with his experience could pick up on the

fact that moisture was gathering between her legs. The scent was being absorbed in his nostrils. He wanted to touch her there. Taste her there, like he was tasting her mouth. Mate with her there, the way his tongue was mating with hers. He was consumed by an urgency, an insatiable hunger.

His hands moved from the wall to grip her hips, then behind her to cup her backside. The soft material of her dress was no barrier against the hard erection he pressed against her. Her fingertips were pressing hard into his shoulders, eliciting pain and pleasure at the same time.

For him, kissing had always been a prelude to the next phase of sex. It was foreplay that he enjoyed, but he knew the prize was when he penetrated a woman, going deep and riding her hard. But with Nikki he had a totally different mind-set. His taste for her was relentless. Never had he craved kissing a woman so.

And to think she had assumed he hadn't enjoyed this the first time around. If only she knew the reason he'd left that day had had nothing to do with not enjoying the kiss but everything to do with enjoying it too much.

And now his insides felt as if they'd burst into flames and the only way to put them out was to take her to the nearest bed and lose himself. With that thought in mind he lifted her into his arms.

The feel of being swept off her feet caused Nikki's senses to return in full force. She pushed against Jonas's chest before easing out of this arms. There was no need to ask where he thought he was about to take her. He'd been headed in the direction of her bedroom. And there was no need to ask how he knew just where the room was located when he'd never set foot in her house before. Men like Jonas had built-in radar when it came to a woman's bedroom. She pulled in a deep breath, thinking that had been some kiss, definitively hotter than the last.

"Do you believe me now, Nikki?"

She glanced up, and like a magnet her gaze automatically latched to Jonas's mouth. Seeing the shape of his damp lips made her lick her own when she remembered why his were wet. Yes, she believed him. After the way he had devoured her mouth, she had no choice but to do so. And the thought that he had enjoyed the kiss as much as she had sent her into a head spin. He was fire and if she thought she could play with him without getting burned then she was only fooling herself. And her mother hadn't raised a fool. To keep her sanity, she needed to distance herself from him as soon as possible.

"You got the kiss so now you can leave." In reality he'd gotten a lot more than that. He'd snatched her common sense right from her, which was why she needed to hurry him out the door.

"Okay, I'll go, Nikki. But if you change your mind about coming on board for the Fulton project, let me know within the week."

She stared at him. Did he honestly think she could work with him now? Whenever she saw him she wouldn't think of work; she would think of kisses.

"There's no way I can work with you even if I had a change of heart, Jonas."

He took a step back and placed his hands in his pockets. "Why not? You're a big girl. I'm sure you can handle a one-night stand."

She frowned. There was no way she would consider such a thing. "That's not the point."

"Isn't it? You said you knew about my type so now let me tell you what I perceive as yours. Although you claim you no longer believe in that fairy-tale nonsense of everlasting love, you're still holding out for it. You want to believe that somehow your lucky number will get pulled and you'll meet a guy who wants to put a ring on your finger, marry you and give you babies. But my question to you, Nikki, is this. Are you willing to live your life and hold out waiting for a possibility? What if it doesn't happen? We both know the statistics. Chances are it won't."

He paused a second and to give her more food for thought, he added, "Just think of all the time you waste waiting for Mr. Right who just might not come at all."

She glared at him. "How can you be so cynical when your parents have been happily married close to forty years, and two of your brothers—who use to be die-hard bachelors—are now married?"

A crooked smile touched his lips. "Easily. I consider my parents' marriage one in a million, which means they beat the odds. And as for my brothers...the jury is still out as to whether their marriages will last. Don't get me wrong, I believe they love the women they married and the women they married love them. But a marriage is built on more than just love, so I'll wait and see if either of them will celebrate any five-year anniversaries."

She could only stare at him, not believing he said such a thing. She didn't know Eli and Stacey that well, but anyone who hung around Galen and Brittany long enough knew they were destined to share their lives together forever. How could he not see it? She knew the answer immediately. He didn't want to see it. He simply refused to do so.

"So there's no reason why you shouldn't enjoy yourself, Nikki. Have fun. If not with me then definitely someone else. But at the moment I'm thinking only of myself and the fun the two of us can have together. Why let life slip you by? You're nearly thirty, right?"

Now that was a low blow, Nikki thought. A man never brought up a woman's age. And before she could take him to task for doing so, he went on to add, "Don't get me wrong. You look good for your age. But time isn't on your side. Neither is it on mine. It happens. Life happens. So we might as well enjoy it while we can."

She crossed her arms over her chest and lifted her chin. She wondered if this was the game he ran on his women who eventually gave in to him. "Is that all?"

"No, but I figured that, along with the kiss, is enough for you to think about for now. However, if after all your reflections you still decide affairs aren't your thing, I still would like to work with you again. I'll even keep my hands and lips to myself and retain a strictly business relationship with you. Like I said at dinner, you're the best photographer around and I need the best for this project."

A smile curved his lips. "Good night and I hope to see you around."

Nikki blinked when the door closed behind Jonas. She then drew in a deep breath, wondering if she had imagined the whole thing. Had she and Jonas actually kissed again?

She touched her lips with her fingertips. They felt

sore and she knew why. This kiss had been more powerful than the last one. Jonas hadn't just kissed her, he had devoured her mouth. And she hated to admit that she had enjoyed it. Immensely. Slowly drawing air into her lungs, she could still taste him on her tongue. Her body was in shock mode with tingling sensations rushing through it. Every muscle was quivering, and she was overheated with want and need that had her insides sizzling.

She moved away from the wall thinking Jonas had read her loud and clear. She wanted to be a bad girl with a good-girl mentality. She even had Brittany convinced that she was a woman with no hang-ups about engaging in casual affairs. The lie had sounded so true that she had begun believing it herself. But Jonas had shown her she was way out of her league.

Okay, he'd told her he was attracted to her, and the kiss somewhat proved that he was. What he hadn't told her was why he had kept his distance for eighteen months.

She rubbed her forehead, feeling a humongous headache coming on, but she knew what she had to do. Tomorrow she would call Senator Joseph's campaign headquarters and accept the offer they'd made. The sooner she got busy with her life, the sooner she could put thoughts of Jonas out of it.

Jacketless, shirtless and horny as hell, Jonas let himself into his house. On the drive home he kept calling himself all kinds of fool for kissing Nikki again. Why was he a glutton for punishment? At least he didn't have to wonder why he was so drawn to her.

There was something about her taste that even now

was causing an ache in his lower extremities. When had a kiss been so overpowering? So downright delicious that his entire body was revving up with thoughts of another one? And then another...

Besides that, there was something different about their date—and whether he wanted to admit it or not, what started out as a business meeting had ended up as a date. He had enjoyed her company more than any other woman's. Mainly because in addition to being a great conversationalist, she had a sense of humor. She had shared with him some of her and Brittany's escapades as teens growing up together in Florida.

What he needed to do was clear his mind and he knew the best way to do it. A way that worked each and every time. Taking the stairs two at a time he entered his bedroom and changed into a pair of jeans and a T-shirt, the perfect outfit for a late-night ride on his Harley.

A short while later he was in his garage, putting a band on his hair to hold the strands together before placing a helmet on his head. He straddled his bike, ready to hit the open road. Adrenaline flowed through every part of his body when he fired up the engine and took off like the devil himself was chasing after him.

He knew the route he was traveling. Could follow it with his eyes closed since it was the same one he always took whenever he rode his bike late at night. This was his favorite time for riding with a big beautiful dark sky overhead and stars sprinkled about. Usually he felt at peace, but on this particular night his mind was in turmoil. He definitely needed this ride.

He settled in his seat, drew in a deep breath and let the adrenaline flow. The sound of the thrumming engine had a calming effect, one he felt all the way down to his bones.

Now if he could only get Nikki out of his mind. A frown appeared between his eyebrows. Why even now, when he was out on the open road in the middle of the night, could he still inhale her scent? And why couldn't he get out of his mind just how she'd looked tonight in that outfit?

His frown deepened. How she looked tonight had nothing on her taste, which was something else he couldn't seem to get over. But he would. No matter what it took. Damn, hadn't he made that same resolution eighteen months ago?

The only reason he'd kissed her tonight was because he'd undergone a moment of temporary insanity. He was convinced that had to be it. And he was equally convinced that by this time tomorrow he would be back in his right mind and in some other woman's bed to make him forget. Hadn't that been what had helped him the last time? Yes, somewhat, but it hadn't taken care of the root of his problem.

He wanted Nikki in a way a man usually wanted a woman. In his bed. Whether he'd admit it or not, kissing her a second time had pretty much changed the dynamics of their relationship. She was now under his skin deeper than before.

Jonas looked ahead and saw the flashing railroad crossings go down. He expelled an agitated breath and brought his bike to a complete stop.

"If you straddle a woman like you do that bike then you're definitely a man who knows how to ride."

Jonas rolled his eyes before glancing at the very attractive woman seated behind the wheel of a canary-yellow Corvette convertible idling beside him. His gaze first appreciated the car and then the woman. The look she was giving him made him feel naked. Unfortunately for her, he didn't experience even the faintest hint of excitement from her intense perusal.

"Yes, I know how to ride and enjoy doing so," he responded, knowing neither of them was talking about his bike.

"Then maybe you need to follow me."

He thought that maybe he did, until he saw the ring on her finger. "And maybe you need to go home to your husband."

She pouted. "He's no fun."

Your problem, not mine. "I don't encroach on another man's territory."

"Um, that's a pity," she said sarcastically.

"Probably is." *Especially since tonight I'd love to ride a woman more than this bike.*

But as he took off when the railroad crossing arms went back up, he knew the only woman he wanted to ride. But he didn't want to think about it. He didn't want to think about her.

So he continued to ride as he tried to shut off his mind to any thoughts of Nikki Cartwright. About to take a curve, he leaned in, liking the feel of power beneath his thighs. It was a thrumming sensation he couldn't get anywhere else. The vibration of the bike's engine helped to lull him into a contented mood for the time being. He felt totally in sync with the road, the bike he was riding, and the entire universe. The feeling was totally awesome.

Jonas tried to recall the last time he'd had a woman on the bike with him. It had been a while since his back had rested against a pair of plump, ripe breasts or a woman's arms had been wrapped around him while she held on tight.

At that moment the image of the only woman he wanted to share a bike ride with loomed in front of him. And he was suddenly filled with arousal that had his erection pressing hard against his zipper. He drew in a deep breath and adjusted his body on the seat. As much as he wished otherwise, it was evident that Nikki would not be eradicated from his thoughts anytime soon. The woman was one sensual piece of art.

It was only when he came to a stop at a red light that he took in his surroundings. He was only a block away from where Nikki lived. What had possessed him to come this way when he lived in the other direction? What was this madness? He should be putting as much distance between them as he could. That kiss was proof enough that when it came to her he couldn't think straight.

And maybe that was the reason he should have a face-off with her once and for all. Granted, Nikki was a challenge to his sensibilities, but he refused to run in the opposite direction whenever he saw her, like he'd been doing for the past eighteen months. He would face her like a man and do what he knew he needed to do and be done with it.

Hell, the way he saw it, he would be doing her a favor. Like he told her, she was approaching thirty and it was time to put all that nonsense of a forever love out of her head. Being a romantic was one thing. Being a hopeless, incurable romantic was another.

He checked his watch. It was late, close to one in the morning. But there was someone he needed to call now.

Pulling to the side of the road, he killed his engine and removed his helmet. He took his cell phone out of his pocket to make a call.

"Hello."

"Stan. I figured you would still be up."

"Jonas? Kind of late for you to be calling. Is there a party somewhere that I'm missing?"

Jonas chuckled. "No. Just calling to collect a favor."

"Okay, buddy. I owe you so many of them I won't waste my time asking which one. Just tell me what you need."

"Your brother Jeremy is campaign manager for Senator Joseph, right?"

"Yes, that's right."

Jonas nodded. "Someone made a job offer to a photographer by the name of Nicole Cartwright. I want them to pull the offer."

"Pull the offer?" Stan asked, surprised.

"Yes."

"All right. I'll see what I can do."

"Thanks. I appreciate it."

Satisfied for the time being, Jonas returned the cell phone to his pocket and put the helmet back on his head. Firing up the bike's engine, he headed for home.

Chapter 5

"Senator Joseph's campaign actually withdrew their offer to hire you as a photographer?" Brittany Steele asked as she gazed across the table at her best friend.

"Yes," Nikki said, still somewhat annoyed at the call she'd received yesterday.

"Why?"

"They said something about reevaluating the budget. It was definitely bad timing since I had planned to call them to accept." Nikki glanced around Samantha's Café where she had met Brittany for lunch. A popular place to dine, the establishment was crowded.

She looked back at Brittany. "Now I need to look at other opportunities. Weddings, anniversary parties and family portraits are nice to do on the side, but they won't pay the bills."

"So what are you going to do?"

After taking a sip of her coffee, Nikki answered, "Not sure, especially since I turned down Jonas's offer."

Brittany raised an arched brow. "Jonas offered you a job?"

Nikki nodded. "Yes. It was a chance to work with him on that Fulton project. And he was going to pay twice as much as the Joseph campaign."

"Then why did you turn down Jonas? I would think being a part of that Fulton project would be a dream come true."

Nikki's cheeks warmed. There were certain things she had withheld from her best friend, and now it was time to come clean. "Do you recall that day we ran into each other when you first arrived in Phoenix and you were bidding on your mother's property?"

Brittany smiled as she cut into her salad. "Yes, that was over a year ago, but I remember. It was short of a miracle that we ran into each other after all those years."

"Yes, and that night we dined at Malone's and played catch-up on what's been going on with us over the past twelve years."

Brittany's smile deepened. "I was stressed out about Galen's outlandish proposal for my mother's property."

"Yes, well, I wasn't completely forthright about a few things."

Brittany stopped what she was doing and stared. "About what?"

"My relationship with Jonas, for starters."

Surprise lit Brittany's features and she set down her fork and knife by her salad bowl. "You and Jonas were involved?"

Nikki chuckled. "Only in my dreams. But when I

brought him up, I made it seem as if the two of us had merely worked together once or twice and hadn't gotten all that close."

"But you and he had been close?"

"Not sexual or anything like that. But we had kissed. The reason I didn't say anything was that I was too embarrassed to admit it, especially since it was a kiss that led nowhere. And one I took more seriously than he did. We were at my office one day and had gotten excited over this deal he'd clinched and got caught up in the moment."

Nikki leaned back in her chair. "Trust me. He regretted the kiss soon enough and made sure he kept his distance whenever we would run into each other after that. In fact, the first time we came in breathing space of each other again was at your wedding."

She could remember that day like it was yesterday. She had been one of the bridesmaids and he one of the groomsmen. She had avoided him like he'd been determined to avoid her.

"And I saw him again when I was the photographer at Eli's wedding," she said, stirring her soup. She shook her head. "It's funny we only seem to run into each other at weddings."

Nikki paused, remembering that day at Eli's wedding. She could have sworn more than once Jonas's gaze had been on her, but when she would glance over at him he would be either engaged in deep conversation with someone or looking someplace else. "I was surprised when I got a call from him three days ago asking that we meet to discuss a business proposition."

"The Fulton deal?"

"Yes. We met, he made the offer and I turned him down."

"Why?"

Nikki met Brittany's gaze. "Because I knew I would not be able to control myself around him…which leads to my next confession."

"Which is?"

"I'm not living in the fast lane like I led you to believe on that night. I gave you the impression that I'd given up believing in a knight in shining armor and that I was independent, empowered, a woman on the move. A woman who wanted nothing more than a casual affair with a man. I wanted to believe I was all those things and had convinced myself I could be. But…"

"But what?"

"I blew a big chance to prove myself with Jonas this week, which leads me to believe that I might not be as ready to move out of my comfort zone as I thought. Deep down a part of me is still programmed to believe in happy endings and everything that goes along with it—love, happiness and commitment. But then there's another part that knows such things no longer exist for most women and that I need to stop reaching for a fantasy and accept reality. I can't have it both ways."

She pushed her soup bowl aside. "So all that advice I gave you that night was all talk, and nothing that I would have had the courage to try myself."

A smile touched Brittany's lips. "All talk or not, it was good advice and if I hadn't taken it, I wouldn't have Galen." She leaned back in her chair and eyed Nikki squarely. "Sounds to me like there's a battle going on inside of you. Your head against your heart. Your head is filled with notions of how today's woman should act and the things she should want, versus the things that your heart—the heart of a romantic—wants. That old-fashioned happy ever after."

Brittany chuckled. "And don't you dare ask me which one you should listen to. That's a decision only you can make, and you'll know when it's the right one."

Nikki shook her head. "Not sure about that, and I might have muddied the waters even more. Jonas and I kissed again the other night."

The expression on Brittany's face showed she wasn't surprised. "And?"

"For me it was better than the first time, and there's no doubt in my mind that he enjoyed it as much as I did. But I know the score, Britt. Jonas is a bona fide player who doesn't have a serious bone in his body."

"And you want to become a female version?"

Nikki shrugged. "Not to that degree, but you know what they're saying. Good men are extinct, and more and more women aren't depending on a man for their happiness."

"*They're* saying. And just who are *they*?"

"Magazine articles, talk shows, reality shows, anybody you ask. Finding love, happiness and commitment is as unlikely as walking down the street and finding a million-dollar bill."

Brittany chuckled. "There aren't million-dollar bills."

Nikki giggled. "See there, another reason not to waste your time looking."

Brittany shook her head. "Seriously, in the end you have to do what makes you happy."

"But what happens if what makes me happy is something not good for me?"

"Then you'll know it and eventually reject it. In the

end, either your head or your heart will win." Brittany paused a second and then asked, "So what are you going to do about Jonas and that job offer? Is it too late to tell him you've changed your mind and want it after all?"

Did she want it after all? Nikki nibbled on her bottom lip. Nothing had changed since two nights ago. She still didn't feel comfortable working so closely with Jonas again. But in reality she realized that something had changed. She no longer had choices with her employment situation. She needed a job.

She was still attracted to him and it seemed he was attracted to her. But for how long? She couldn't forget his reputation when it came to women. "Not sure what I'm going to do yet. To go back and tell Jonas that I've changed my mind and will work for him is easier said than done. The issues I had with it then are the same issues I have now. And it wouldn't hurt if he wasn't so cynical."

Brittany laughed. "Yes, he's definitely that. I love my brothers-in-law, but they're hard-core players. However, look at Galen and Eli—so were they once. So maybe there's hope."

Nikki didn't know about the others but figured that hope was on the other end of the spectrum when it came to Jonas. However, at some point she needed to see it as his problem and not hers. She had allowed his way of thinking and acting to rain on her parade, and that wasn't fair. She should not have been afraid of taking that job for fear of how she would act based on his actions.

She sighed upon realizing she had turned down what could have been her big break because of him. Instead of taking his offer and taking him on in the process, she had given in to her fears and backed away.

She glanced up at Brittany and took a deep breath. "My financial needs outweigh my emotional ones right now. And you're right. It will be a battle between my head and my heart. I just hope I can survive the fight."

3 days later

"Mr. Steele, Nikki Cartwright is here to see you."

Jonas looked up from the document he was reading when his secretary's voice came across the intercom. *Finally,* he thought. It had taken Nikki almost a week to come calling, and for a minute he'd gotten worried that perhaps he'd misplayed his hand and there was some other job she had lined up that he hadn't known about. He tossed what was left of his Tootsie Pop in the trash can by his desk, leaned back in his chair and smiled. Evidently that wasn't the case.

"Give me a few minutes to wrap up this report, Gail, and then send her in," he said, standing to straighten his tie. He didn't have any report to wrap up. He needed the extra time to prepare himself mentally for the woman he couldn't get out of his mind. He sniffed the air; he inhaled her scent already.

He checked to make sure his shirt was neatly tucked into his pants while thinking that he would discount the fact it had taken manipulation on his part to get her here. After their second kiss, it had become extremely clear to him just how much he wanted Nikki in his bed, and at that point he had decided he would do whatever it took to get her there. Sleeping with her once should do it. He was convinced of it.

He was marveling over the brilliance of that supposition when he heard the soft knock on his office door. "Come in."

His gaze connected with hers the moment the door opened. He swallowed tightly and immediately thought he might need to sleep with her more than once. It would be breaking a rule, but some rules were made to be broken. "Nikki, this is a surprise." Like hell it was. He'd been expecting her. Hoping she would take the bait and decide she needed to work for him after all.

"I hope I didn't catch you at a bad time, Jonas. I thought about calling but figured it would be best if we talked in person."

"Sure, have a seat."

He watched her cross the room to the chair he offered, and thought she looked fresh in her jeans and pretty blue blouse. He liked how the denim fit over her soft curves. Seeing her in a dress that night had taken the guesswork out of what her legs looked like, and he hated that she'd covered them up today.

"You can have one of those," he said of the Tootsie Pops in a candy jar on a table near Nikki's chair.

"No, thank you. I don't normally have a sweet tooth."

He had to bite back from saying sweet tooth or not, what he'd tasted of her so far was simply delicious. He went to sit on the edge of his desk to face her, inhale her scent, recall the fantasies he'd had of her just last night. They'd been hot, lustful, erection-throbbing fantasies of him riding her. Her riding him. Oral sex. Can't-walk-the-next-day sex. When his stomach clenched he figured he better get his thoughts under control and out from under the bedcovers.

"So what can I help you with, Nikki?"

She began nibbling on her bottom lip, which meant she was nervous. He felt his erection throb, which meant he was horny. With effort, he pushed from his mind the thought of just what those two things might have in common.

"The other night you offered me the chance to work with you on the Fulton project."

He nodded slowly. "Yes, and you turned me down."

She looked good today, sexy as hell. Innocent and hot all rolled into one. There was something about that curly hair of hers and the way it crowned her face. It teased the primal maleness inside of him. And that errant curl that seemed to always be out of place, falling just so between her brows, was hammering something fierce below his belt.

"Yes, but later you said you would hold the offer for at least a week, in case I changed my mind," she reminded him.

He held back from telling her he didn't need reminding. He knew just what he said, how he'd said it and why he'd said it. It was right after deciding, that whether he liked it or not, eighteen months hadn't rid him of his desire for her and he would risk any feelings of vulnerability that bedding her would bring on. The main thing was to get her out of his system so things could go back to normal for him.

"Yes, I did say that. So, have you changed your mind, Nikki?"

"Yes. Does that mean the job is still available and you'll consider me for it?"

"Like I told you, I want the best and I consider your skill with a camera unsurpassed." That was the truth and had nothing to do with his plan to get her in his bed. The bedding part was a done deal as far as he was concerned.

"Thanks." She began nibbling on those lips again and there was silence between them. There was more she wanted to say, he knew, but she was hesitating.

"I take it that there's something else you need to clear the air about before you make your final decision." He couldn't let her sit there and gnaw her mouth off. He couldn't afford for her to do that, not when he had plans for that luscious-looking mouth of hers.

She sat up straight in her chair. "Yes, there is. We've kissed. Twice now."

He nodded, fighting back the urge to tell her that was for starters and didn't come close to all the other things he intended for them to do now that he'd made up his mind about a few things regarding her. "Yes, that's twice now."

"It can't happen again. You did say you're willing to keep your hands to yourself."

Yes, he had said that. But that didn't necessarily mean he'd meant it. "Is that what you want?"

He'd seen it. She hadn't been quick enough to disguise that flash that had appeared in her eyes. He knew what it meant so whatever she said now didn't matter one iota.

"Yes, that's what I want."

Yeah, right. "Okay, I'll give you what you want." And he meant every word. She was going to discover soon enough that a hands-off policy between them was the last thing she really wanted.

He pushed away from his desk. "So, are you going to work for me?"

When she hesitated, he lifted a brow and a smile

touched his lips. "What? Do you need me to put the strictly business policy in writing or something?"

She stood as well. "Of course not."

"Then what is it?"

"Nothing."

He tilted his head. "I think there is something bothering you."

She adjusted the straps of her purse on her shoulder. He couldn't resist breathing in her scent and almost groaned.

"No, I'm fine."

You definitely are. "If you're sure, we can shake on it for now and then Gail will have your contract ready in a few days. Like I told you there's a launch party to attend in Las Vegas."

She nodded. "I'll be there. I just need the itinerary."

"Gail will call you when that's prepared as well."

He crossed the room to her, refused to consider the very real fact that he hadn't been completely honest with her about everything and that she probably wouldn't like it one damn bit when she found out how he'd manipulated things to get what he wanted.

Jonas reached his hand out to her and she took it, and he immediately felt his body's reaction to the feel of her smaller hand in his. "Welcome aboard, Nikki. I'm looking forward to working with you again."

He knew she felt something as well, although she was struggling hard not to. She tried not to make eye contact with him. Tried not to glance down at their joined hands. "Thanks, Jonas."

When she began nibbling on her lips again he figured it was time to release her hand. "You still have my mobile number, right?" he asked.

"Yes."

"Use it to contact me if you have any questions. I'm attending a wedding this weekend in New York, and from there I'm flying out for Vegas." A smile touched his lips. "I plan to have a little fun in Sin City before work begins."

He saw another flash that flitted in her eyes before she had time to hide it. Um, was the mention of his fun time in Vegas causing her worry? Should he take that as a red flag that the forever-after side of her had a tendency to show every once in a while? Hell, he hoped not since that sort of thinking was a waste of time with him.

"Enjoy yourself."

His grin was mischievous. "I intend to."

She tilted her head slightly and the mass of dark curls hid one eye so he couldn't completely figure out what she was thinking. "We'll be in Vegas a few days before flying to Los Angeles," he said while leading her to the door. "That's where we'll board the *Velocity*. And from there our two-week adventure begins."

What he didn't add was how much he was looking forward to that time. He intended to work hard and play even harder. "Any questions, Nikki?"

She shook her head. "No questions. I'll see you in Vegas, ready to work."

Every muscle in his body reacted to the thought of them working closely together. In the conference room. In the bedroom.

Chapter 6

Nikki clutched her hand to her chest as she stared out the taxi's window. For as far as her eyes could see, there were tall elegant hotels, neon signs, glitter and glitz. Sin City. She could just imagine all the transgressions being performed and knew all of it wasn't at the slot machines. She shook her head. What had she expected from a state where prostitution was legal?

"Your first time in Vegas?"

She glanced up at the driver. Truth be told, it might be her last time as well. She was feeling overwhelmed. "Yes, and I doubt I've ever seen anything like it."

She figured there was no decline in the economy here, at least there shouldn't be. The casinos never closed. And just how many Elvis impersonators had she seen since leaving the airport?

"You haven't seen anything yet. Just wait until this

place lights up at night. That's when everything looks spectacular."

She could only imagine. Twice in the past she'd made plans to come to Vegas, but each time those plans had fallen through for some reason or another, leading her to believe there was a bad omen between her and this city.

Nikki didn't want to consider the possibility that her being here now didn't bode well, either. She had gotten a call from Jonas's secretary a few days ago letting her know there had been a change and she was needed in Vegas earlier than originally planned. In addition to rearranging her schedule, she had rushed to do some shopping to make sure she had all the appropriate outfits she would need beside her usual jeans and blouses. She couldn't help wondering what turn of events had made Jonas decide she needed to be here ahead of her scheduled time.

As the cab continued to whisk her along the Vegas Strip, a part of her tried downplaying her excitement in seeing Jonas again. She should really get over it—and him, to boot. Wasn't he the same man who'd kissed her twice already and then told her he planned to leave for Vegas a few days early to have fun—no doubt with other women? Not that she thought those kisses had meant anything to him, mind you. But it was the principle of the thing.

But that's just it, Nikki. Men like Jonas have no principles. When will you finally see that?

She let out a frustrated sigh. It's not that she didn't know it, because she did. It was her heart side—the one still filled with idealistic hopes and dreams—working against her, refusing to accept what her head already knew *but just refused to accept on most good days*.

She looked down at the camera around her neck and was reminded of the real reason she was here. It wasn't about Jonas. It was about her doing a good job and making a name for herself. If she didn't succeed at this project she would have no one to blame but herself.

But still…

And there was that *but* in there, although she wished otherwise. There was nothing wrong with enjoying herself while she was here, if time allowed. Her brother always said if you work hard then you should reward yourself and play harder. Truthfully, she couldn't recall the last time she'd had some "let your hair down" fun. Maybe it was about time she did.

Nikki settled back against her seat's cushion. She had a feeling that before she left Vegas she was going to have an eye-opener as to just how sinful this city really was.

Gannon Steele stared across the hotel room at his brother. "Now tell me again why Nikki Cartwright is arriving in Vegas earlier than planned?"

Jonas rolled his eyes as he continued to button his shirt. He wasn't surprised the youngest of the Steele brothers was questioning why he'd sent for Nikki to come to Vegas early. Gannon was pouting, disappointed that the two of them wouldn't be hanging together as originally planned. That meant Gannon would have to visit some of the Vegas hot spots on his own, including the Doll House, a gentlemen's club owned by one of Galen's friends, Quinton Hinton.

Gannon, who'd turned thirty a few months ago, was

determined not only to blaze a trail for himself, but also to follow in his older brothers' footsteps by doing the wild and the reckless. Over the years Gannon had heard about their outlandish escapades and exploits, and figured what was good for the goose was also good for the gander.

"I told you already. She needs to get set up, and I need to make sure Fulton knows we're on the job," Jonas replied.

"Yes, but her flying in means you'll be working and really, man, nobody comes to Vegas to work."

"I did, and you knew that when you followed me here, so stop whining."

Gannon frowned. "Hell, I'm not whining."

Jonas rolled his eyes. "Yes, you are, so get over it already or I'll send you back home to Mama."

Jonas chuckled when he saw Gannon's frown. Brother number six hated being reminded he was the baby in the family. Jonas loved his youngest brother, but at times he really wondered about him and hoped to hell he didn't end up being the worst of the lot where women were concerned. Their mother would never forgive them if he did. Gannon was still easily influenced by his older brothers and Eden had accused them more than once of corrupting Gannon's mind.

If only she knew. Gannon might be the youngest and he might be impressionable, but he could hold his own in ways Jonas didn't want to even think about. Back in the day there was no such thing as social media. And now Gannon had taken internet dating to a whole new level. Hell, he had even come up with his own form of speed dating.

"Checking out one of those brothels is on my to-do list today."

Jonas nodded. He wasn't surprised and figured that visiting one of those would probably make Gannon's day…and probably his night as well. He wouldn't complain if it kept Gannon busy for a while and out of his hair. "Sounds like a good plan. And I'll give Quinton a call to let him know you'll be dropping by the Doll House sometime later and to make sure you have a good time."

Gannon's face lit up. "Hey man, that will be great. I appreciate it."

Jonas chuckled. "Hey, that's what brothers are for."

It was only after Gannon left that Jonas took a moment to sit down, unwrap a Tootsie Pop and stick it in his mouth as he reflected on the real reason he had asked Nikki to come to Vegas early. As much as he assumed he would have fun in Sin City, he'd discovered that instead he had spent his time thinking about her, counting the days, the hours—hell, even the minutes—when she was to fly in. And for a man who was usually on top of his game, he hadn't been involved with any woman since the night they kissed. He hadn't a desire to do so. Hell, what was that about?

Instead of heeding these red flags, he took an even deeper plunge by summoning her earlier. At one point it was as if he couldn't get her here fast enough. He was tired of waking up from dreams in which she had a leading role and which had left him hornier and even more frustrated. He could only smile at the depth of his manipulations. He'd seen it as the only way to take care of those pent-up frustrations that had begun taking over his senses. If things went as planned, his photographer would be arriving any minute.

In all honestly, he had lied. There was nothing they needed to do before the launch party, but there was definitely something he needed to do. Bed her. Get her out of his system. And do it sooner than he'd anticipated.

He checked his watch. He would give Nikki time to rest up from her flight and then he would seek her out.

Nikki brushed back a curl from her face as she glanced around the spacious hotel suite. Decorated in the most vibrant colors and prints, it was simply beautiful. She hadn't expected a suite. A standard room in this hotel would have been enough considering the hotel's extravagance. But she had no complaints and liked the fact that Ideas of Steele was being more than generous.

She had a sitting room separate from the bedroom, which had a bed that was bigger than any she'd ever seen. *Leave it to Vegas,* she thought. But what really caught her eye was the flower arrangement on the coffee table. Thinking it was a gift from the hotel, she crossed the room and pulled off the card.

Nikki, welcome to Vegas. We need to have dinner later to go over a few new developments. I'll call you. Jonas

Her brow furrowed. *New developments?* Placing the card on the table she headed toward the bedroom to unpack, certain she would find out soon enough just what those new developments were.

A short while later, after she had unpacked and

taken a shower, she stood looking out the huge floor-to-ceiling window in the sitting room. Already she was anticipating nightfall when she would see the Strip light up. She figured she should have an awesome view from her suite on the thirtieth floor.

She tightened the belt of her bath robe—courtesy of the hotel—and was about to go back into the bed-room when the hotel phone rang. Crossing the room, she picked it up. "Yes?"

"Nikki, this is Jonas."

She drew in a deep breath. Why did he have to sound so darn sexy? And why did the fact that that sexy voice also belonged to a man with a sexy body and a drop-dead gorgeous face have her heart beating like crazy in her chest? She didn't even have to close her eyes to envision the tall, dark and handsome mass of sensual masculinity on her phone. Just once she would love to run her fingers through his wavy hair, nibble at the cor-ners of his lips before sliding her tongue between them.

Feeling overheated and knowing those thoughts were out of line, she cleared her throat. "Jonas, thanks for the flowers. They're beautiful."

"You're welcome and I'm glad you like them. I felt it was the least I could do for having you come out sooner than we discussed. I appreciate your flexibility."

"No problem. You mentioned something about new developments."

"Yes. I'll cover everything over dinner. Is six o'clock okay?"

"Six will be fine. Do you want us to meet in the lobby?"

"No, I thought we could have dinner in my suite."

She paused and immediately the intimate setting

flashed right before her eyes and sent feathered sensations down her spine. She forced her heart to stop pounding while she tried to restrain her thoughts. The thought of just the two of them in his hotel room was—in addition to everything else—causing heat to form between her thighs.

"Nikki?"

Girl, get that head of yours out of the gutter. Can't you tell by the sound of his voice he's all about business and nothing else? He's gotten two kisses off you and figures that's enough, so chill. He hasn't been the least bit unprofessional since you and he agreed on your terms. He probably wants to have an early dinner with you so he'll have time for some hot date later tonight.

"Yes, I'm still here," she said, finally responding to her name

"Will dinner in my hotel room at six work for you? If not, I could squeeze some time in for us to go out if you prefer."

Squeeze some time in? Please. Don't do me any favors. "Dinner in your suite will work fine, Jonas. That way I can get out and tour the city later." She stayed on the line long enough to get his room number before hanging up.

She glanced at her watch. She had four hours and figured she might as well take a nap. After she had dinner with Jonas she would take a stroll down Las Vegas Boulevard. It was bound to be a long night and she wanted to be well-rested.

Jonas paced his hotel room while sucking on a Tootsie Pop. He glanced at his watch again. He had another fifteen minutes and he didn't know any woman who would arrive early to anything, so why was he tripping?

Oh, he had an easy answer for that one. He wanted Nikki. Now if the evening would only go according to his plans. They would enjoy dinner and then enjoy each other—all night long. He was no longer worried about the outcome of any type of vulnerability on his part. Since seeing her in Phoenix he had convinced himself he was dedicated to bachelorhood, and there was no woman alive who could make him think differently, no matter how deep his desire for her went.

Then what was with the flowers, Steele?

"So okay, I sent them," he muttered under his breath to the imaginary mocking voice he heard in his head. He had played on her romantic side in sending those flowers but didn't feel the slightest bit of regret doing so. When it came to women the only time he played fair was when she belonged to someone else.

So as far as he was concerned, the lines were free and clear with Nikki. A few months ago, without giving anything away, he'd gotten Galen into a conversation about her, figuring Galen and Brittany probably told each other everything. He'd been right.

Although Galen didn't know a whole hell of a lot, he was positive Nikki wasn't seriously involved with anyone. Jonas had figured that much out on his own after they'd kissed that first time. And the second time, he hated to admit he hadn't really thought about whether she'd gotten involved since then or not. Her dating status had been the last thing on his mind that night when he'd all but begged her for that kiss.

He paused in his pacing to toss the finished pop

in the trash. And speaking of that kiss—hell, not just one but both—he couldn't get it out of his mind. It didn't take much to remember the feel of her enticing curves plastered against him while he took her lips with a hunger that he could remember even to this day, at that very moment. His gut clenched and his heart began beating like crazy in his chest. There had to be a reason he wanted her so badly, and why even now his heart was racing while he waited for her arrival.

He was about to start pacing again when he heard the knock on his hotel room door. He checked his watch and saw Nikki was seven minutes early. His mother, who was the epitome of punctuality, was seldom early. She would use every single minute to make sure she was well together, as she would say.

Inhaling deeply he moved toward the door, feeling the way his heart was kicking with each step he took. He tried to prepare himself, figuring he was making a big deal out of nothing. Nikki probably wasn't wearing makeup—not that she needed any. More than likely she was wearing jeans—although he thought she looked good in them, too. And chances were she had her camera around her neck since he'd only seen her without it a few times.

He opened the door and swallowed deeply as his gaze ran all over her. She was wearing makeup, a skirt that showed off her beautiful legs, and instead of a camera, she had a beaded necklace around her neck.

She looked simply gorgeous.

Chapter 7

"You did remember we had a meeting, didn't you?" Nikki asked Jonas when he stood there and stared as if he hadn't been expecting her. He was wearing dark dress slacks and a crisp white shirt, as if he was about to go out for the evening.

"Of course. What makes you think otherwise?" he asked, stepping aside for her to enter.

"You're all dressed up."

His gaze roamed her up and down, then returned to her face. "So are you."

No, she wasn't really, she thought, glancing down at herself. Little did he know the few times she did get dressed up, she cleaned up pretty well. "I'm checking out the Strip after our dinner meeting."

He closed the door and leaned back against it. "You do that a lot, don't you?"

She lifted a brow. "Do what?"

"Go out alone. Why? I'm sure getting dates isn't an issue for you."

They'd had this conversation before so why was he bringing it back up again, she wondered. Evidently he'd forgotten their discussion. "I like male company, don't get me wrong, but once in a while I like just doing things solo. I don't have to impress anyone or—"

"Play the kind of games you think men like me are so good at playing," he broke in to say.

So he had remembered. "Um, yes, something like that." Not wanting to get into a debate with him about the tactics he used with women and just what she thought of them, she glanced around. "I thought my room was nice—thanks, by the way—but this one is even nicer. But that's expected since you're *the man*."

"Am I?"

She grinned. "Yes, my bank account will definitely proclaim such in six weeks."

He threw his head back and laughed. The sound was both surprising and heartwarming, sending hot shivers escalating up her body. In addition to the busy zipper on his pants, it seemed Jonas knew how to let down his hair and he had enough locks on his head to do it. "Glad to know I'm doing my part to stimulate the economy," he said when he finally stopped laughing.

She fought back the urge to tell him that he was doing his part in stimulating other things as well. Like that inner part of her that was feeling arousing sensations just from listening to his voice. And her eyes were appreciating the sight of him as well. His slacks covered muscled thighs, long legs and a trimmed waist, and his shirt couldn't conceal well-defined abs and broad shoulders.

She drew in a deep breath and then released it slowly. "Your note said something about a new development, which is why you wanted me in Vegas earlier than planned."

"Yes, we need to talk about that. Dinner will be here any minute."

She followed him to the sitting room, and when he gestured to the sofa, she sat down. Then she watched him ease his body into the chair across from her. He picked up a folder from the coffee table. It was then she noted the bag of Tootsie Pops. Evidently he liked the things.

"It's nothing major, just a change in how we're presenting *Velocity* this weekend," he said. "We're still providing the brochures as planned, but I've come up with something I think will add dimension to our presentation."

"What?"

"The use of JumboTrons, strategically located at different places in the ballroom, running simultaneously to give attendees an idea of what to expect when they board the *Velocity.*"

She immediately envisioned such a thing in her head and could see it working to their benefit. "But will we have time to work on the video?"

"Yes, my videographer, Rick Harris, is in Los Angeles now, putting together everything on his end. It'll arrive on Friday. I'd like you and Rick to make sure everything is ready by Saturday night's launch party."

He paused a moment and then asked, "What do you think of that idea?"

"I think it's fantastic. Rick and I have worked together before on other projects and he's good."

Adding those JumboTrons really wasn't a big deal and wouldn't account for her having to drop everything and fly in to Las Vegas three days earlier than planned. There had to be more "new developments" they had yet to discuss. She tilted her head to the side and gazed over at him. He had unwrapped one of those Tootsie Pops and placed it in his mouth.

The muscles between her legs clenched at the way Jonas was sucking on the lollipop. You could tell he was getting sheer enjoyment out of doing so. And there was something about how the pop was easing in and out of his mouth, being worked by his tongue, leaving a sweet glaze all over his lips.

He caught her staring and held her gaze. "Would you like one?"

She swallowed. "No, thank you. Is there anything else to discuss?"

He shook his head and put the unfinished pop aside. "No, that's about it."

"You seem to like those," she said, motioning to the bag of Tootsie Pops on the table in front of him.

Jonas smiled. "Yes, they have definitely grown on me. They started out as a supportive measure from my brothers when I quit smoking some years back. They figured the pops would replace the cigarette. Basically they have."

He checked his watch. "Dinner should be here soon."

Nikki nodded. If the JumboTrons were the only new development then her coming to Vegas early made no sense, especially when Rick wouldn't be arriving until

Friday. That meant she had two whole days to do practically nothing.

She was about to point that out to Jonas when there was a knock on the door. He stood. "I'll get that. I think that's our dinner."

Jonas took a deep, steadying breath while watching Nikki leave to go to the powder room to wash her hands. He had seen the look in her eyes when she'd asked if there were any other new developments. She was an intelligent woman and was probably wondering why he'd sent for her three days before she was actually needed. Adding those JumboTrons was no big deal. She knew it as well as he did.

"Will there be anything else, sir?"

He glanced over at the waiter who had wheeled in the table set for two. "No, that will be all," he said, signing the invoice.

He was closing the door behind the man when Nikki returned. "Whatever it is smells good," she said.

Not as good as you smell and look, sweetheart, he thought, turning around and scanning her up and down. He really liked that outfit on her, admired the way the material clung to her hips and her rounded bottom and accentuated her curves. And then there were the shoes she was wearing. The sling backs did some serious business to her shapely legs.

He then recalled what she'd said earlier about walking the Strip after their dinner. Not by a long shot. Little did she know he had plans for her after they ate. Um, he could easily switch the timing of those plans to before dinner without much hassle. The food would keep and they would definitely have worked up an appetite for it later.

"I took the liberty of selecting something off the menu. I hope you don't mind. I understand you're a seafood lover and shrimp is your favorite."

"Yes, that's right. How did you know?

A smile touched his lips. "That's my secret."

He decided not to tell her he made it his business to know about any woman in whom he was interested. However, he would admit he had taken more interest in finding out things about her than any other woman before.

Before she could ask him to divulge those secrets, he said, "Now it's my turn to wash my hands. I'll be back in a minute."

Nikki watched Jonas walk away. All the Steele men had a sexy walk—even the old man—but she thought Jonas's was the sexiest. And the way his shoulders moved while the thick wavy hair flowed around his shoulders was eye-catching. She had never thought she would be attracted to a man who had more hair on his head than she did, but Jonas had proved her wrong.

He had also proved her wrong about something else as well—that she couldn't want him any more than she had before. And that surprised her, especially after that pep talk she'd given herself on the plane and most recently the one she'd had before stepping onto the elevator that had brought her to his penthouse suite. The look on his face when he had opened the door had reminded her of that night at Mavericks, when he had stared at her that same way.

She must be imagining things, especially since

they'd reached an agreement. And they had reached an agreement, hadn't they? He would be keeping his hands to himself. No more kisses, no more intense attractions or talk of an affair, right? Then why did she feel he was stripping her naked with his gaze each and every time he looked at her? And why was she stripping him naked with hers? Her mind was envisioning what he was packing underneath his slacks and shirt. And why did she want to see it for herself just for the hell of it?

She drew in a deep breath, not believing the way her thoughts were going tonight. But then why was she so surprised? Brittany had warned her about the battle—her head versus her heart. Her head wanted Jonas, the man, with all his flaws. Even if it was just to say she'd gotten a taste of the forbidden and was able to enjoy it and move on.

But her heart was singing another song—one of Love and Happiness—and intended to give Al Green a run for his money. Her heart didn't want her to waste her time on a man like Jonas, a man who could take that same heart, if given the chance, and break it. A man who would get what he wanted and then walk away without looking back.

Her heart wanted more. It felt it deserved more, and although there was no sign of a Mr. Right out there for her just yet, her heart didn't want her to give up too soon.

"Ready?"

She blinked upon realizing Jonas had returned. When she felt intense heat stir the lower part of her belly, she tore her gaze away from his, thinking of all the things she could be ready for. Those mesmerizing green eyes had an unnerving effect and were messing with her mind. They were hypnotic, spellbinding and luring her not to think straight.

"So are you going to stand over there, or will you join me over here, Nikki?"

The impact of his question had her staring at him. They were still talking about sharing dinner, weren't they? Then why were emotions she always downplayed around him suddenly forcing their way to the forefront? Confusing her mind? Suffusing her with heated warmth at the juncture of her thighs?

Nikki slowly crossed the room to where he stood beside the table. She had thought he would pull out the chair for her, and when he just stood there and stared at her, she felt her heart almost racing out of control. He moved and stepped closer, not just to crowd her space but to get all into it and take command. Hot shivers flowed through her.

And why was he wearing the scent of a man, a sensual aroma that was inebriating her senses? Her heart was being pushed to the background, where only her head was speaking, and what it was saying wasn't good. Definitely not smart.

Get real, girl! You claim you want to make the transition from a woman who believes in fantasies to a woman who realizes the real fantasies are the ones you make for yourself. There are no knights in shining armor, just rogues in aluminum foil. At least you know where this one stands and there won't be any expectations on your part. Cross over to the desire side by doing a smash and grab. Smash what has proved to be idealistic baloney once and for all, and grab what could be an experience of a lifetime.

She swallowed, hearing all the things her head was saying, but still, when he took a step even closer, her heart fought back and she couldn't stop the words. "If I remember correctly, things were going to be strictly business between us, Jonas."

A smile curved his lips. "Um, that's not how I remember things."

She narrowed her gaze. "And just what do you remember?" His scent was driving her crazy, breaking down her defenses even more.

He inched closer, and she felt him, his aroused body part pressed against her middle. Instead of recoiling from it, she felt fire rush through her veins and race up her spine. That same head that was trying to fill her mind with naughty thoughts began spinning. It was kicking out her common sense and replacing it with a whole lot of nonsense. Making her wonder such things as how it would feel to slide her fingertips along that aroused member, cup him in her hand, taste him in her mouth and—

"I distinctively recall a promise to give you what you wanted," he said, interrupting her thoughts and lowering his head down to breathe the words across her lips. "And I intend to push you over the edge, Nikki Cartwright, and make sure you want me."

And when he captured his mouth with hers, she knew she didn't stand a chance because she was a goner the minute he slid his tongue inside her mouth.

Chapter 8

Jonas had developed a taste for Nikki from their first kiss. That had to be the reason he was taking her mouth with an urgency that was stirring all kinds of emotions within him. It didn't matter that her mouth felt like pure satin beneath his or that her lips were a perfect fit. The only thing that mattered was the way they were connecting so intimately to his as he sank deeper and deeper into the warmth of her mouth.

Tangling with a woman's tongue had never driven him to the point where lust ruled his senses. The fire that had built up inside of him was blazing out of control, and that was the one thing he never lost with a woman. Control. And he knew at that moment there was no way he could regain it.

There was nothing he could do to stop the flow of adrenaline that was rushing through his body, drowning his pores and playing hell with his molecules. And his erection was throbbing fiercely, sending a sensual warning that if he didn't pull back now, there would be no pulling back later.

If he didn't ease his shaft inside of her, penetrate her deep while she moaned, thrust in and out and make her cream all over him, he would lose his mind. He wanted to make love to her so badly he could hardly stand it, and the thought of doing so sent shivers through him.

What he felt wasn't just desire, it was hard-core desire. And he refused to waste his time trying to figure out why. He'd done so for eighteen months and still didn't have a clue.

He continued to kiss her as if her tongue had been created just for him to enjoy. And he could tell she was enjoying it too from the way her fingertips were digging into his shoulders. Her moans sounded so starkly sexual they were tapping into his emotions, both physical and mental, and he knew of no way to stop them.

The need to breathe made him break off the kiss, and he stared up at her while every muscle in his body tightened in yearning. "I suggest that you tell me to stop now, Nikki, because if you don't, I plan to mate with you all over this place."

He paused a moment and then decided to add, "And just so you'll know, when I finish with you, the last thing you'll have energy for is a walk down Vegas Boulevard."

He'd been so brutally honest, but he felt that she deserved to know what she was up against. He had a fierce sexual appetite, and with her it would take a long time to be appeased. There was something about her that was tempting everything male inside of him. And there could only be one possible outcome.

Jonas watched the rise and fall of her breasts as she tried getting her breathing under control. He saw by the V-neckline of her shirt that she was wearing a pink bra. He couldn't help wondering if her panties were pink as well. That curiosity had him shifting his gaze back to her eyes and what he saw in them almost made it difficult to breathe.

Although she might never admit it to him or to herself, she wanted him as much as he wanted her. There was no if, and, or but about it. The eyes looking back at him were full of fire. As much fire as he felt thrumming through his loins right now. And at that moment, he planned on making good on what he'd told her. He intended to push her over the edge. Right onto her back with him on top.

He leaned in and slanted his mouth over hers again. His hands moved from her waist, slid down to cup her bottom and squeezed it gently before bringing it closer to the fit of him. Without releasing his hold on her mouth, he shifted to bring his hard erection closer to the juncture of her thighs, eliciting an automated sigh from deep within her throat. He liked the sound.

And he especially liked how she arched her back, bringing the firm tips of her breasts into his chest like heated darts, and sending shock waves of pleasure riveting through him. He felt hot inside and was burning in places that had never burned before. He moved closer, needing her curvaceous body even closer to his.

This time she was the one who pulled back from the kiss. But before she could draw in a quick breath he was unbuttoning her shirt as swiftly as his fingers could move to do so, trying like hell not to rip any in his haste. She hadn't told him to stop so he planned to make good on his threat. There was no way he could walk away from this, from her, even with all those red warning signs flashing him all in the face.

Without wasting time he went to the front clasp of her sexy, pink lace bra and unhooked it, freeing the most luscious-looking breasts he'd ever seen and soliciting a growl that erupted from deep in his throat.

His hands went still as he lifted his gaze from her breasts to her eyes. It seemed as if time stood still as their gazes connected, held, fused in a way that just wasn't rational. But at that moment, he couldn't break eye contact even if he wanted to.

Silence surrounded them and the air seemed electrified, charged, pricked with an element so sensual, the components were unknown to mankind. There was this unexplained and undefined chemistry between them. They'd gotten primed, ready, saturated in lust, and there was no turning back. No letting mere kisses suffice any longer. No more denying what they both truly wanted, although they should be fighting it. That was no longer an option. They wanted the real deal and wouldn't waste any more time getting it.

Nikki hadn't expected this, an odd surge of passion that splintered everything within her—every logical thought, every ounce of common sense. Instead she was feeling a burst of freedom that she'd never felt before and it was rejuvenating her all through her bones. She wanted this. She wanted him. She no longer cared that her head was winning the battle and her heart was losing this round. The main thing was that there was another war going on inside of her and it had nothing to do with logic, and everything to do with need.

And what she needed at that moment was to make love with Jonas. No matter how many regrets she might have in the morning, she needed him to touch her, make love to her all over the place just like he'd threatened to do. So she stood there and watched him. Waited with bated breath.

Now she understood the reputation he had attained. In the confines of the sauna rooms, ladies' clubs and sorority meetings, the feminine whispers discreetly echoed around town that when it came to lovemaking, bad-boy Jonas Steele had a finesse that could be patented. She'd never doubted it then, and she was seeing it in action firsthand now.

He slowly lowered his gaze to travel down her body, and she felt the heat of his green orbs on her breasts. Her hardened nipples seemed to tighten even more before his eyes. She felt it and knew he had to be seeing it.

"I need to suck on them, Nikki. I need to let my tongue wrap around them. I need to lick them."

His words broke the silence and suddenly the air oozed with need. A need that was unbearable and fueled by a lusty craving. Her gaze followed the masculine hands that reached up to push both her shirt and bra from her shoulders, bearing the upper part of her breasts to him. From the look in his eyes, he more than liked what he saw.

Before he could make a move she decided to play the Jonas Steele game by reaching out and all but snatching the shirt off his body, ripping buttons in the process and ignoring the fact that replacing the shirt would cost a pretty penny. At the moment she didn't care.

Nikki saw the tattoo on his stomach, a huge, raging bull. It was appropriate since he had the stamina of one. She was tempted to lick his stomach to soothe as well as tame such a fierce-looking animal. Then she would move lower and let her tongue wrap around him like he planned to do her.

Do her.

The thought of him doing her made the juncture of her thighs cream. And she felt the thickening moisture drench her panties. She tightened her legs together as sensations flared in her womanly core.

If he was surprised by the way she'd torn the shirt from his body he didn't show it. It seemed he was just as pushed over the edge as she was. And like her, he had inwardly conceded there was no turning back. No more discussions. From here on out there would only be action.

Her head had taken over big-time, filling her mind with thoughts of doing him, and acting out the part of the vixen she'd bragged to Brittany she was but had never truly been. She suddenly wanted to see if she could handle the role.

"You've done it now, sweetheart."

His words, laced with hot caution, spoken in that deep baritone of his, didn't scare her any. If anything they sent shivers of anticipation racing through her body at the same time they kicked her courage and confidence levels up a notch.

Before Nikki could dwell on anything else, Jonas reached out and pulled her to him in a way that had them tumbling to the carpeted floor, though he made

KIMANI
ROMANCE

An Important Message from the Publisher

Dear Reader,

Because you've chosen to read one of our fine novels, I'd like to say "thank you"! And, as a special way to say thank you, I'm offering to send you two more Kimani™ Romance novels and two surprise gifts— absolutely FREE! These books will keep it real with true-to-life African American characters that turn up the heat and sizzle with passion.

Please enjoy the free books and gifts with our compliments...

Glenda Howard
For Kimani Press™

eel off Seal and

Place Inside...

We'd like to send you two free books to introduce you to Kimani™ Romance books. These novels feature strong, sexy women, and African-American heroes that are charming, loving and true. Our authors fill each page with exceptional dialogue, exciting plot twists, and enough sizzling romance to keep you riveted until the very end!

KIMANI ROMANCE...LOVE'S ULTIMATE DESTINATION

All I Want is YOU
DARA GIRARD

PRIVATE Luau
Devon Vaughn Archer

MAUREEN SMITH
ROMANCING THE M.D.
HOPEWELL GENERAL

SEDUCTION AT WHISPERING Lakes
LINDA HUDSON-SMITH

Field of PLEASURE
FARRAH ROCHON

Your two books have combined cover price of $12.50 in the U.S. $14.50 in Canada, but are yours **FREE!**

We'll even send you two wonderful surprise gifts. You can't lose!

2 FREE BONUS GIFTS!

absolutely FREE

www.ReaderService.com

THE EDITOR'S "THANK YOU" FREE GIFTS INCLUDE:

Two Kimani™ Romance Novels
Two exciting surprise gifts

▶ Detach card and mail today. No stamp needed. ▶

YES! I have placed my Editor's "thank you" Free Gifts seal in the space provided at right. Please send me 2 FREE Books, and my 2 FREE Mystery Gifts. I understand that I am under no obligation to purchase anything further, as explained on the back of this card.

EDITOR'S
FREE GIFT SEAL
THANK YOU

168/368 XDL FMQS

Please Print

FIRST NAME

LAST NAME

ADDRESS

APT.#   CITY

STATE/PROV.   ZIP/POSTAL CODE

Thank You!

Offer limited to one per household and not applicable to series that subscriber is currently receiving.
Your Privacy—The Reader Service is committed to protecting your privacy. Our Privacy Policy is available online at www.ReaderService.com or upon request from the Reader Service. We make a portion of our mailing list available to reputable third parties that offer products we believe may interest you. If you prefer that we not exchange your name with third parties, or if you wish to clarify or modify your communication preferences, please visit us at www.ReaderService.com/consumerschoice or write to us at Reader Service Preference Service, P.O. Box 9062, Buffalo, NY 14269. Include your complete name and address.

The Reader Service - Here's How It Works:

Accepting your 2 free books and 2 free gifts (gifts valued at approximately $10.00) places you under no obligation to buy anything. You may keep the books and gifts and return the shipping statement marked "cancel." If you do not cancel, about a month later we'll send you 4 additional books and bill you just $4.94 each in the U.S. or $5.49 each in Canada. That is a savings of at least 21% off the cover price. Shipping and handling is just 50¢ per book in the U.S. and 75¢ per book in Canada.* You may cancel at any time, but if you choose to continue, every month we'll send you 4 more books, which you may either purchase at the discount price or return to us and cancel your subscription.

*Terms and prices subject to change without notice. Prices do not include applicable taxes. Sales tax applicable in N.Y. Canadian residents will be charged applicable taxes. Offer not valid in Quebec. All orders subject to credit approval. Credit or debit balances in a customer's account(s) may be offset by any other outstanding balance owed by or to the customer. Offer available while quantities last. Books received may not be as shown. Please allow 4 to 6 weeks for delivery.

If offer card is missing write to: The Reader Service, P.O. Box 1867, Buffalo, NY 14240-1867 or visit www.ReaderService.com

BUSINESS REPLY MAIL
FIRST-CLASS MAIL   PERMIT NO. 717   BUFFALO, NY

POSTAGE WILL BE PAID BY ADDRESSEE

THE READER SERVICE
PO BOX 1867
BUFFALO NY 14240-9952

NO POSTAGE
NECESSARY
IF MAILED
IN THE
UNITED STATES

sure his body cushioned her fall. Trying to regain the breath that had been snatched right from her lungs, she glanced down at him at the same moment she realized she was sprawled on top of him, her limbs entwined with his. She was shirtless and her skirt was hiked high enough she could feel air hitting her almost bare bottom. She felt her womanly core react to the hard erection pressing against it.

"Kiss me," he rasped before pulling her mouth down to his and immediately sliding his tongue between her lips. Sexual energy between them was surging out of control and she felt it in the sensual mating of their mouths.

Her senses were overwhelmed with the scent and feel of him at almost every angle. Their bodies writhed against each other, as if they couldn't get close enough, and his hands lifted her skirt even higher to palm her backside. His fingers traced a sensuous path along the crevice as if to verify she was actually wearing a thong. And then he released her mouth to latch on to a nipple, sucking it between his lips the way she'd seen him do that Tootsie Pop earlier.

Nikki moaned deep in her throat and felt her inner muscles contract with the sucking motion of his mouth on her breasts. He wasn't just trying to taste her, he was consuming her and propelling her body into quivers that rammed all through her. She had made love before, but never like this and never with this intensity or greed. And what frightened her even more was knowing there was pleasure still yet to be fulfilled. Areas yet to be discovered.

She moaned again when his mouth moved to her other breast, sucked another nipple between his teeth as if his very life depended on it. And now his hands were no longer torturing her bottom but had traveled to the front, eased between their connected bodies, slid underneath the waistband of her thong to begin toying in her now drenched feminine folds, stirring up the air with her scent.

He suddenly released her breast and gave her only a second to see the smile that curved his lips before he flipped her on her back so she was staring up at him. Before she could blink he had removed the shoes from her feet, and proceeded to jerk her thong and skirt down her hips and toss them aside, leaving her completely bare. Naked as the day she was born.

She held her breath as his gaze roamed up and down her body from head to toe, and she actually felt the hot path his gaze took and knew what areas it concentrated on before moving on to another. Then he was lifting her legs, hoisting them high up on his shoulders and bringing his face up close and personal to her bikini-cut feminine mound.

He leaned forward and she felt intense heat from his nostrils when he took his nose and pressed it against her, rubbed it up and down in her as if to inhale her scent as deep into his nasal cavity as he could. And then his nose was replaced with the tip of his tongue that jabbed through her folds, straight for her clit.

His mouth latched on to her, and then it was on. Every single rumor she'd heard whispered about him and his deadly steady, lickity-split, seemingly mile-long tongue was true. The man definitely knew how to give pleasure while he enjoyed the ultimate feast. Somehow he seemed to close his mouth in a way that made his jaws lock on her as his tongue greedily devoured her like it was a treat he'd developed a sweet tooth for, a craving he couldn't get enough of.

Never had she been sensually mauled this way before. Never had any man used his tongue to pleasure her to this degree. His tongue went deep, stroked hard, and she couldn't stop the moans as tension built within her, making her already electrified senses reel.

"Jonas!"

She screamed his name when her body fragmented into tiny pieces with the most intense climax she'd ever experienced. Instead of letting her go, he slid his hands beneath her, lifting her hips, pressing her more firmly to his mouth while his greedy tongue possessed her mega-stimulated mound. The sensations surging through her were over the top, off the charts, mind-boggling and earth-shatteringly explosive.

And before her heart rate could slow down, he quickly shifted positions and pulled her up in front of him, on her knees with her back to him. She heard the sound of him tearing off the rest of his clothes and ripping into a condom packet with his teeth.

Before she could recover from the orgasm that still had her mind reeling, her teeth chattering, he grabbed hold of her hips, spread her thighs and proceeded to slide his hard shaft into her from behind.

She continued to shudder as he began riding her, locking his hips to hers with every hard thrust. The sound of flesh beating against flesh as his skin slapped hard against her, his testicles hitting her butt cheeks, made her senses start reeling all over again. He glided his hands under them and cupped her breasts as he rode her. Each stroke into her body was long, sure and done with a purpose and not a wasted effort.

And when she threw her head back and tilted her hips at an angle to give deeper penetration, Nikki heard Jonas's deep groan before he frantically bucked against her body while using his hands to keep the lower part of her locked tight against him.

"Nikki!"

At that moment she didn't want to think of how many other names he'd screamed or that she would be added to the list. Another notch on his infamous bedpost. What mattered most at that moment was that they were in sync, connected with his engorged sex planted deep within her womanly core while her inner muscles clenched, relaxed and then clenched mercilessly again, draining him like he was draining her. He was once again showing her just how hot and explosive lovemaking could be, and she felt deep satisfaction all through her bones.

She came again as fire consumed her, raged out of control and compelled her to cry out his name once more as she enjoyed every last moment of the experience. And before she could fully recover, she felt him pulling her up off the floor and gathering her into his arms.

"Now I'll feed you and then we'll do this all over again in my bed."

And she knew at that moment he would make good on his warning that before he was finished with her they would do it all over his suite.

Chapter 9

The ringing of the hotel room's phone stirred Jonas from a deep and peaceful sleep. He slowly opened his eyes and squinted against the bright sunlight shining in through the window. It took a split second to recall where he was and why his body felt so achy. He couldn't stop the smile that touched his lips when the memories of the night before came flooding through his hazed mind.

He glanced at the spot beside him and saw it was empty. Except for the ringing of the phone there wasn't another sound. He didn't need to be told he was alone and his bedmate of the night before had vanished. Pulling up in bed, he reached out to answer the phone. "Yes?"

"Hell, I was about to hang up. What took you so

long to answer? I tried calling your cell phone all night. Where the hell were you?"

Jonas rubbed his hand down his face, frowning at all the questions Gannon was firing at him. "The reason it took me so long to answer the phone was because I was asleep," he growled.

"And the reason you couldn't get me last night was because I was busy." That was all his brother needed to know. There was no way he would admit that he'd been trying to screw Nikki's brains out. Which made him wonder how she had gotten out of the hotel room. After the intensity of their lovemaking, he was surprised she could still walk.

"Well, since you're up you can join me for breakfast. I can't wait to tell you about all that went on at the Doll House."

Jonas rolled his eyes. Gannon might be bursting at the seams, but personally, he could wait. Besides, he was very familiar with the gentlemen's club so nothing Gannon told him would come as a surprise. "I'm not up yet, Gan, so do breakfast without me. I need at least another three hours of sleep."

"Uh-oh. That means you scored last night. I have a feeling you didn't sleep in your bed alone and probably aren't alone now."

Jonas had no intention of appeasing Gannon's curiosity about his sexual activities, especially when they involved Nikki. "Goodbye, Gannon. I should be well-rested by lunchtime."

"I'm visiting that brothel today."

Jonas shook his head. "Make sure you have plenty of condoms."

"Dammit, Jonas, I'm not a kid. I know how to handle

my business, thank you very much. Just make sure you're handling yours."

Jonas blinked when the sound of Gannon's phone clicked loudly in his ear. He drew in a deep breath. Okay, the kid was thirty now, but old habits were hard to break. The five of them were so used to looking out for their baby brother they sometimes forgot he was now a man. And Jonas had to constantly remind himself that he was only two years older than Gannon. Two years but with a hell of a lot more experience.

He glanced around the room. One thing was for certain: Gannon was right, he needed to take care of his own business. And the first thing that topped the list was Nikki. The first order of business was to find out why he'd awakened alone in bed this morning. He was usually the one to decide at what point a woman left his bed and couldn't recall when it was ever the other way around.

But then he couldn't ever recall having sex with any woman with the intensity of last night's session. Nikki had drained him dry. He hadn't stood a chance against the contractions of her inner muscles. He had come more times than he could remember and had been putty in her hands. But then, she'd also been putty in his. He couldn't recall the last time he'd enjoyed getting between a pair of spread legs so much. And they hadn't been just any woman's legs. They had been Nikki's.

And then there had been his obsession with tasting her. He had gone down on her more times in a single night than he'd done all year. It seemed that once he'd tasted her, he hadn't been able to get enough. It was as if her clit had been created just for his mouth. At least his tongue had evidently thought so. Even now he was convinced the taste of her had lingered, and a part of him was glad that he could taste her again. He licked his lips and found her there. His curly-headed, jeans-wearing, tasty-as-hell fantasy girl.

He closed his eyes, not wanting to think of any female as being his fantasy girl. He hoped like hell that last night had effectively cleansed his desire for her from his system and that he wouldn't get hard each and every time he thought about her.

He frowned. If she was out of his system then why were shivers racing through him at the thought of seeing her and making love to her again? And why couldn't the memories go away? The memories of him on top of her. Her on top of him. Their bodies mating, moving together in an urgency that took his breath away just thinking about it. The feel of being inside of her, and how her inner muscles would clench him tight, while he took her with a hunger that bordered on desperation and greed.

He shook his head, trying to free himself of the memories and saw that he couldn't. The vision of her naked body, the intense look on her face when she came and the sound of her letting loose in pleasure were things he couldn't forget, so there was no use trying.

But he knew he eventually would forget when he moved on to another woman. He frowned at the thought that he didn't want another woman right now. He liked her well enough and there was no reason to move on. Surely one more night with her wouldn't hurt anything. A powerful force of pleasure rushed through him at the thought.

He would grab a few more hours of sleep and then he would get up, get dressed and get laid.

* * *

As the sunlight slashed its way through the curtains, Nikki lay in bed and stared up at the ceiling. Each time she moved she felt aches from muscles she hadn't used in years. But thanks to Jonas, she had certainly used them last night.

Granted she'd only made love but twice in her entire life—once in college and the other when she'd thought she'd met the man of her dreams four years ago, only to find out he'd shown interest just to make his old girlfriend jealous. She'd thought both times were okay, decent at best. However, what she'd shared with Jonas last night went beyond decent. In fact, there was nothing decent about any of it. They'd gotten downright corrupt. Never in her wildest dream had she expected to share something that naughty with any man. Did couples actually go that many rounds, try out all those positions even on a good night? She'd never experienced anything so amazing, so hot and erotic. And so spine-tingling sensational. Her dreams and fantasies hadn't come close to the real thing.

She remembered how she had checked out his body, studied all his tattoos. She had liked the fierce-looking bull on his stomach, but her favorite had been the Libra sign on his side.

She pulled in a deep breath thinking he had certainly given her fair warning. Nothing could have been closer to the truth. She wondered if other men had that much energy and enjoyed sex that much. And she knew that's what it had been, nothing but sex. He hadn't made love to her. She had made up her mind to stop equating sex with love.

So where did that leave her?

She knew the answer to that one. It left her right where she had lied about being for the past two years. She could remember the day she had looked herself in a mirror and decided to give up on marriage and babies and instead join the ranks of the single ladies. There was no man out there to put a ring on it so she'd decided to live her life, have fun and not have any regrets.

She closed her eyes to fight off the regrets. She really shouldn't have any. Any other woman would be smiling this morning from ear to ear. But then, any other woman probably would not have sneaked out of Jonas Steele's bed and fled to her own hotel room, where she'd slid into bed and eased her overly sore body beneath the covers.

Now it was morning and she was awake, her body still sore, and her heart fighting a losing battle against the memories stored in her head. And they were memories that made her blush just thinking about them.

After having sex that first time—on the floor of all places—Jonas had planted her naked body into the chair to eat dinner. And then he proceeded to sit across from her—naked as well—while they ate. He had carried on a conversation with her as if it was the most natural thing to share dinner with a woman in the nude.

Probably a natural thing for him, but it had definitely been odd for her. At least it had been at first. That was before dessert time when he had crawled under the table to where she sat, told her to spread her legs and then used his tongue on her like she was an ice cream cone, slowly licking her before plunging in deep with long, penetrating kisses. She had lifted the tablecloth to look down, observing the way his mouth was paying very special attention to that part of her, watching how he would flick his tongue left to right, right to left and then to the center before gently scraping against her clit with his teeth. Moments later, she couldn't help but lean back in her chair and stretch out her legs to spread them farther apart while he made her moan and groan. Never had she experienced anything so scandalous.

Nikki closed her eyes and drew in his scent, which wasn't hard to do since he'd left an imprint on every inch of her. She couldn't stay in bed all day. Besides, she knew from her workout classes at the gym that the best way to ease soreness out your body was to get a move on.

She glanced out the window. It was daytime now, but last night she had seen the brightly lit Strip from Jonas's hotel room. She had stood at his window. Well... actually, she had been leaning toward his window while he'd gotten her from behind.

Knowing if she continued to lie there she would eventually drown in all those tantalizing memories, she moaned at her sore body as she eased out of bed.

She would take a shower, get dressed and do what she had planned to do last night but had not gotten around to doing. She would walk the Strip.

"Just who do you keep trying to call, Jonas?"

"None of your business." Jonas frowned, putting his cell phone back in his pocket as he glanced across the table at his brother.

They were sitting downstairs in one of the hotel's restaurants waiting on the waitress to bring their food. He had slept five hours instead of the three, and would have slept longer if Gannon hadn't called, waking him up again.

Gannon smiled. "Yeah, right. You found another woman and you're trying to make a hit, aren't you?"

Jonas stared at his brother as he took a sip of his lemonade. Gannon would probably fall out of his chair if Jonas admitted he was trying to make a hit on the same woman from last night. He seldom did repeats and most people knew it. It wasn't in his makeup to spend time doing just one woman. Not when there were so many of them out there to do.

Instead of answering Gannon, he asked, "You've spent most of the time talking about the naughty happenings over at the Doll House. I noticed you didn't have much to say about your visit to the brothel."

"I haven't gone there yet. I got sidetracked with Nikki."

Jonas swung his head around so fast it was a wonder his neck hadn't snapped. He stared over at Gannon. "Nikki?" He was grateful Gannon had pulled out his iPhone to check messages, otherwise there was no way he would have missed what Jonas knew had to be an intense look on his face.

"Yes, Nikki," Gannon said, studying his phone. "You know, Brittany's best friend. Your photographer who flew in a couple days early because you needed her to start work." Gannon glanced up. "Well, I hate to tell you but she wasn't working today."

Jonas arched his brow, forcing his features to an expressionless state when he asked, "What was she doing?"

"Shopping. Walking the Strip. Having lunch. Shopping some more."

Jonas tilted his head to the side and stared at his brother. "And how do you know this?"

Gannon shrugged as he placed his phone back in his pocket. "I ran into her on the Strip and we spent some time together. I helped her carry her bags and later we had lunch together at The Glades."

Jonas frowned so hard he was certain anger lines appeared in his face. "You had lunch with Nikki?"

"Yes, and if you're getting mad because I woke you up to have lunch again, it was because I was still hungry. You aren't the only one who might have worked up an appetite last night. I met this woman at the Doll House and she was something else."

Jonas glared. Little did Gannon know that his anger had nothing to do with the fact that Gannon was making a pig out of himself by eating two lunches. His anger solely rested on the fact that he'd been trying to reach Nikki and hadn't been able to do so. Was she deliberately avoiding his calls?

"Did Nikki say what she would be doing after lunch?"

Gannon rolled his eyes. "Jesus, Jonas, give the woman a break. Do you really expect her to be on the time clock 24/7? When we parted she was on her way to do more shopping."

He simply stared at his brother knowing Gannon didn't have a clue as to his real interest in Nikki and that was a good thing. He picked up his water, took a sip and tried to ask as inconspicuously as possible, "So, how was she?"

"Who?"

Jonas let out a frustrated breath. "Nikki."

"Oh." Gannon then gave him a rakish smile. "She looked good as usual. Those tight jeans hug that rounded backside of hers like nobody's business."

Jonas frowned, not liking the fact that Gannon had been ogling Nikki's backside.

"Oops. I better not let Mercury hear me say that.'"

Jonas lifted a brow. "Say what?"

"Anything about Nikki's body." Gannon chuckled. "He told me at Eli's wedding that she was off-limits, so I can only assume our brother has the hots for her. He's probably already scored."

At that moment the waitress returned with their food and Jonas wondered if Gannon noticed the steam coming from his ears.

Jonas felt his jaw tighten as he stepped off the elevator onto the thirtieth floor. He hadn't been able to end lunch with Gannon quickly enough. The good thing was that Gannon had been in too much of a hurry to get over to that brothel to notice Jonas's bad mood. Or too busy helping himself to the steak Jonas had ordered but had been too pissed to eat.

He had tried calling Mercury, but according to his brother's secretary, he was in a meeting. But Jonas wanted answers and if he couldn't get them from Mercury, he would get them from Nikki. If she thought she was playing him and his brother against each other she was sorely mistaken. If she was involved with Mercury then why in the hell had she slept with him last night? The one thing the Steele brothers didn't do was share women.

He knocked on her hotel room door. Hard. Inwardly he told himself to calm down, but he was too angry to do so. If he had known something was going on between her and Mercury he would not have touched her. Dammit. Now he couldn't help but wonder when had she'd become involved with his brother. Had it been before or after their kiss eighteen months ago?

The door opened and he saw the surprised look on her face. "Jonas? Is anything wrong?"

He leaned in the doorway, drew in a deep breath and stared at her without saying anything for a moment. Then he silently asked himself why he was there. He had never run behind a woman, gotten upset when he couldn't reach one after a night of sex. It'd always been out of sight and out of mind for him. He'd found it so easy to move on to the next woman.

So why had he gotten so pissed at the thought he hadn't been able to reach her today? And why was the thought of Mercury having dibs on her eating away at his gut? He shouldn't even be here without first talking to Mercury to find out what was going on. But he couldn't wait. He had to see her. He had to know the truth.

"Jonas?"

"What?"

"I asked if anything is wrong."

The urge to reach out and pull her into his arms and kiss her was overpowering. He straightened and tightened his hands into fists at his side. He needed to know if she was involved with his brother. "Yes, something is wrong."

Instead of asking him what, she took a step back to let him into her hotel room.

Chapter 10

Nikki stared across the room at Jonas. He'd said something was wrong, which meant there could be only one logical reason for him to seek her out. Swallowing deeply, she asked, "Did Fulton not like the idea about using the JumboTrons?"

He stared at her for a second, and then instead of answering he rubbed his hand down his face. He then stared at her again and it appeared his green eyes had darkened in anger. "Well, is that it, Jonas?"

He shook his head. "Do you think I'm here to talk about JumboTrons, or that I'm here to discuss business period?"

She really didn't know how to respond to his question, or what answer he was looking for. So she asked a question of her own. "What other reason would you be here?"

He stared at her for a moment. "I slept with you last night," he all but growled.

She wondered what that had to do with anything. He was a Steele. He slept with women all the time. "And?"

"And you were gone this morning and I haven't been able to reach you all day."

She lifted a brow. He had tried reaching her? Why? "My phone battery was dead. I had it on the charger all day. So what's wrong? Why were you trying to reach me?"

He stared at her for a moment and then shrugged. "Doesn't matter now. I need to ask you something."

"Okay. What?"

"Why didn't you tell me that something is going on between you and my brother?"

She stared at him, wondering where he'd gotten an idea so ridiculous. She then recalled she had run into one of his brothers while walking the Strip and he'd offered to help her with the bags she'd collected from shopping. Afterward they'd had lunch together. Had someone seen them together and jumped to the wrong conclusions?

"Gannon was merely kind enough to help me carry a few packages," she said. "Then we—"

"I'm not talking about Gannon," he said in a low voice that was as hard as nails.

Now she knew he really had lost it. "Then what brother are you talking about?" she asked.

"Don't you know?"

"If I knew I wouldn't be asking," she responded smartly.

He paused a moment, narrowed his gaze and then said, "Mercury."

She expressed disbelief in her features. "Mercury! I barely know him."

"Are you saying the two of you are not involved?"

She placed her hands on her hips and glared at him. "That's exactly what I'm saying. Where did you get such a crazy idea?"

"He told someone you were off-limits."

"Then whoever he told that to must have misunderstood." She sighed, shaking her head. "You actually thought I'm banging your brother and still slept with you last night?"

"I honestly didn't know what to think."

Her frown deepened and she lifted her chin. "In that case, it's nice to know the kind of woman you think I am. Please leave."

Jonas stared across the room at Nikki suddenly feeling lower than low. It didn't take much to see she was pretty damn mad. And he could also tell his accusation had come as a blow. He could see the hurt in her face although she was trying like hell to hide it.

He drew in a deep breath when he thought of what he'd all but accused her of. He had listened to Gannon, who'd evidently heard Mercury wrong like she'd said. And instead of waiting to talk to Mercury about it first, he had stormed up here to Nikki's hotel room and confronted her about something that was undoubtedly not true. He couldn't blame Gannon for relaying false info. He could only blame himself for acting on it the way he had.

"I'm sorry," he said, knowing she had no idea the degree of his remorse. He had been quick to think the worst, mainly to disprove this theory that there was something about her that was different from other women he'd messed around with.

"Is there a reason you're still standing there?"

He met her gaze. Held it for a long while before saying, "I'm here because I can't think of being anywhere else."

She stiffened her spine and lifted her chin. "Then think harder while my door hits you in the back."

Boy, she was cruel, but no crueler than he'd been to her with his accusations. "You won't accept my apology?"

"Right now I don't want anything from you. Not even an apology." She paused for a second, drew in what he knew was an angry breath and then asked, "Do you know what your problem is, Jonas?"

Not waiting for him to answer, she said, "You want to judge every woman on the basis of your own sleazy behavior."

He couldn't say anything to that because maybe he probably did. And he wasn't even offended that she thought his behavior was sleazy. It had been described as worse on more than one occasion. Knowing there was nothing he could say or do to redeem himself at the moment, he crossed the room, and before reaching the door, he turned and looked back at her. The intensity of her glare had burned a hole in his back, he could feel it. But he would make it up to her.

Without saying anything else, he opened the door and walked out of it.

Jonas had made it to his room when his cell phone went off and he saw it was Mercury. He answered it in a frustrating voice. "Mercury."

"Hey, Jonas, Nancy said you called. Don't you have

enough to do in Vegas without trying to keep up with me? I hear Gannon visited the Doll House yesterday and that you missed all the fun."

Jonas frowned, not wanting to talk about anything with his brother but Nikki. "Look, Mercury, I want to know about Nikki."

"Nikki?"

"Yes, Nikki Cartwright. Did you or did you not warn Gannon she's off-limits?"

There was a brief pause, and then Mercury said, "Yes, I warned him off."

Jonas's stomach twisted, and it was like the breath had been sucked from his lungs. According to Nikki she and Mercury weren't involved. So did that mean Mercury was interested in her but she just didn't know it? "So you're interested in her?"

Mercury chuckled. "No."

"Then why in the hell would you tell Gannon she is off-limits?"

"Because she is. But I'm not the one who wants her."

Jonas's jaw hardened. "Then who the hell wants her?"

"You do."

"What?"

He could hear Mercury laughing. "Oh yeah, *you* do. I noticed it first at Galen and Brittany's wedding. You couldn't keep your eyes off her when you thought no one else was looking. And then at Eli's wedding when she was taking all those pictures, you were taking her in, angle by angle, every time that cute little body of hers moved around the room. You were all but salivating."

Jonas frowned. "I hate to burst that overimaginative mind of yours, but you're wrong."

"Umm, I don't think so, and now after this phone conversation, I know so. So the way I see it, telling Gannon and Tyson that Nikki was off-limits was actually doing you a favor. You can thank me for it later."

He heard the click as Mercury ended the call.

Nikki stood at the window looking out at the Strip, drawing in deep breaths and then expelling them slowly, tasting the anger still lodged deep in her throat. A part of her still couldn't believe it. The man who had passionate sex with her last night had stood in the middle of her hotel room less than ten minutes ago, all but accusing her of sleeping with one of his brothers? Just because he'd heard Mercury had said she was off-limits? Of all the ncrve. If her career wasn't on the line she would pack up and return to Phoenix in a heartbeat.

But then again, when it came to Jonas, she never thought with her heart. She couldn't. She always thought with her head and that's where the trouble lay. Her head was trying to tell her he'd been more jealous than pissed, but with Jonas that didn't make any sense. Hc could have any woman he wanted. He'd certainly gotten her last night and big-time. And why had he seemed upset when he hadn't been able to reach her today? What was that all about?

She shook her head. Jonas, jealous over her? She chuckled, knowing nothing could be further from the truth. So they had shared lusty, heated, make-you-holler sex last night, through most of the night. For her it might have been a night to remember, but she figured for him it was business as usual.

When she recalled how he had stared her down, accusing her of being involved with his brother, she couldn't help but feel a resurgence of anger. But she needed this job, so the best thing for her was to do what she was being paid to do and leave everything else alone. Jonas fell in the category of everything else.

Okay, she would be a notch on his bedpost, but then he would be a notch on hers as well. Her notches may not get carved as often as his, but she could deal with that. What she couldn't deal with was an involvement with Jonas, so the best thing to do would be to keep her distance.

And that's what she intended to do.

Chapter 11

Jonas's gaze sought out Nikki the moment he walked into the launch party. She had her camera in hand, as she moved around the room and worked it like the professional photographer that she was. Even though she was only wearing a pair of silky-looking slacks and a matching blouse he thought she stood out over all of the women dressed in expensive designer gowns.

Although this was a working event for her, she looked just as elegant and refined as anyone else. And those slacks she was wearing showed what a curvy little backside she had, just as much as her jeans always did. Which was probably why several men were ogling her as she moved around the room, shifting, twisting and bending that cute rounded bottom all around, snapping one picture after another.

One man in particular was Curtis Rhinestone, a reporter for CNN. Jonas and he had attended college together in Michigan and had been frat brothers. He could recall that back in the day while at the university, more than once he and Curtis had competed for the same girl. And now he didn't like the way Curtis all but licked his lips while staring at Nikki. It wouldn't take much for Jonas to cross the room and bust those same lips with his fist.

He drew in a deep breath wondering why it bothered the hell out of him to think of Curtis—or any other man for that matter—checking out Nikki. Why even now the temperature in the room seemed to have risen a few degrees since he'd seen her, and why while looking at her fully clothed he vividly recalled her naked. Beneath him…on top of him…

He took another sip of his drink. Why was he so fixated on her? Hell, she was just a woman. And he'd slept with more than he could ever count. But he'd always had the ability to move on without any problems. Why was moving away from Nikki causing him so much grief? Why couldn't he get a friggin' handle on those emotions she could so effortlessly stir within him?

"Well, if it isn't Jonas Steele."

Jonas looked up into the face of a woman by the name of Chastity Jenkins. He had met the PR firm owner while on a business trip to L.A. three years ago. He'd found her first name amusing since there was no part of her that came with a lock of any sort. It had been a one-night stand and that was all it was ever meant to be. He had made that clear in the beginning and at the end. So he had been surprised at the call he'd gotten a few months later saying she would be visiting Phoenix and preferred crashing at his place instead of a hotel.

As nice as he could, he'd told her he really didn't give a damn what she preferred, but staying at his place, even for a few days, wasn't going to happen. She hadn't liked his response and after expressing that dislike in a few choice words, she hadn't contacted him since.

"Chastity," he said dryly. "It's been a while."

She smiled up at him. "It wasn't my choice, Jonas."

No, it hadn't been her choice. Her comment let him know she still hadn't gotten over things. At least someone hadn't. He glanced over at Nikki. She hadn't looked his way since he'd arrived, which meant evidently she had. The realization annoyed the hell out of him.

Chastity began talking, namely about her favorite subject. Herself. He really wasn't listening, only pretending he was since for the moment, he didn't have anything else to do.

Click.
Click.

Nikki moved around the room, taking pictures of one celebrity after another. This was her first assignment where so many famous people in the same place. And when it came to smiling for the camera they weren't shy.

She fought to ignore the kicking of her heart, which signaled Jonas was somewhere in the room. They had avoided each other for the past two days and that had been fine with her. They'd had their one-night stand—as brief and meaningless as it could get—and had moved on. The decision had evidently been a mutual one. But they did have to work together, so they couldn't avoid each other forever.

She twisted and bent her body, snapping one picture

after another and as if her camera was responding to the call of the wild…and the reckless: it unerringly zeroed on him. She sucked in a deep breath when he was captured within the scope of her camera's lens. Oh, God, he looked good in his dark suit with his hair flowing around his shoulders.

Her camera continued to snap away, as it moved all over him, from his expensive leather shoes to those fine-as-a-dime muscled thighs beneath his slacks. And it didn't take much for her to recall how those same thighs had held her within their tight grasp while riding her.

Her camera continued snapping, moving upward to Jonas's broad chest and the designer jacket he was wearing, to the handsome features that still haunted her dreams. They were dreams she couldn't restrict from her mind. She knew she was taking more pictures of him than any other person there tonight. It was as if she couldn't help it. And then as if he suspected he was the object of someone's attention, he shifted his gaze from the woman he was talking to and looked straight into the lens of her camera.

She swallowed deeply and her mind suddenly scrambled when she felt the full-fledged intensity of his stare directly on her. She forced herself to stay unruffled because she had no reason to lose her composure. She was merely doing her job. Besides, instead of looking at her, he should be concentrating on the woman he was talking to—the one with the heavily made-up face, over-the-top weave job, way-too-long French-tipped nails and blood red lips. She was talking a mile a minute, and all but demanding his attention. Would she be the one to share his bed tonight? The one who would be scratching his back this time? Getting the ride of her life? And should Nikki even care? Her heart began pounding viciously and she knew she cared although she shouldn't.

"Hey, you've been at it long enough. Shouldn't you be ready to take a break about now?"

She turned toward the deep, masculine voice and couldn't help but force a smile. It was the same guy who'd tried hitting on her earlier. He'd introduced himself as Curtis Rhinestone and said he worked for CNN. It was as if he'd singled her out since she had felt the heat of his gaze on her most of the night. He wasn't bad-looking. In fact most women would probably consider him downright gorgeous. She would too, if he could in some way hold a candle to Jonas. Unfortunately, he couldn't.

She lowered her camera, thinking she'd focused on Jonas too much already. She checked her watch. "You're in luck. Starting now I'm free for the rest of the night."

He smiled. "Good. I think it's time we got to know each other."

Out of the corner of his eye Jonas watched Nikki move around the room with Curtis and felt his anger rising. How dare Rhinestone try to take something that was his?

He drew in a sharp breath. When had he ever thought of any woman as his? No matter how many women he bedded, he'd never claimed one. What made Nikki different? What had there been about having sex with her that still had him breathless? He took a sip of his drink, his last for the night, as he continued to track

Nikki and Curtis while trying not to be too damn obvious.

"Excuse me if I'm boring you."

He shifted his gaze back to Chastity. Why was she still there, taking up his time? A better question to ask was why was he letting her? He knew the reason. He was allowing her to do so because she was so into herself she wouldn't notice that he was into someone else. At least he figured she wouldn't notice. Evidently he'd been wrong.

"You aren't boring me," he said, taking another sip of his drink.

"Then why are we still here? The last time we attended a party together we'd left within minutes."

She didn't have to remind him. They'd split the party in L.A. and he'd taken her up to his hotel room. He was just about to respond, explain that it had been three years ago, tons of women ago…especially one in particular. But then he saw Curtis lead Nikki outside on the patio and knew he had to put a stop to *that* foolishness once and for all.

"It was good seeing you again, Chastity. Now if you will excuse me…" Not waiting to see if she would excuse him or not, he walked off.

"It's a beautiful night, isn't it?"

The cool air hit Nikki in the face as she glanced over at Curtis. He was nice enough and for the time being, had taken her mind off Jonas, which was a good thing. Whether she liked it or not, the sight of Jonas and that woman who kept touching his arm, batting her false lashes up at him while giving him a toothy smile, had irked her. So when Curtis had suggested they step out on the patio, she had been more than raring to go.

She glanced around. They were high up on the fortieth floor, where she could see the brightly lit Vegas Strip with all the flashing neon signs. "So you're going to be a passenger on the *Velocity*?"

She smiled up at him. "Yes, and you will, too. Right?"

"Yes, I'm doing the coverage for CNN and looking forward to the next two weeks."

She took a sip of her wine. "So am I. Although I'll be working a lot of the time, I'll have time to relax and enjoy myself."

He smiled down at her. "And I hope I'll be someone that you'll enjoy your leisure time with."

Nikki wasn't caught off guard by his suggestion. In fact, she had been preparing herself for it. For the past twenty minutes he had been tossing out hints that he would love to spend time with her. The man sure didn't know the meaning of taking things slow.

"Are you sure you want to do that?" she asked.

"I'm more than sure. You're a very sexy woman and any man in his right mind would want to show you a good time."

In the bedroom, of course, Nikki thought. *Been there, done that just three days ago, and the memories are still too potent for me to even consider doing it with another man anytime soon...or ever.*

She was about to open her mouth, to tell him that she wasn't sure that was a good idea, when a masculine voice behind her spoke up.

"I don't know how that will be possible, Rhinestone, when she's with me."

Nikki spun around so fast she almost spilled her drink. She drew in a deep breath and watched as Jonas emerged from the shadows and strolled into the light. The muscle that was ticking in his jaw indicated he was angry, and if looks could kill both she and Curtis would be dead. What was his problem, and why had he made such an outrageous claim just now?

"Steele, I wasn't aware she was with you tonight."

Curtis's words jerked her from her dazed moment. What was Jonas trying to pull? She wasn't with him. He knew good and well that they didn't have that kind of relationship.

She was about to open her mouth to say just that when Jonas came to stand beside her and said in a voice with a hard edge to it, "Well, now you know."

Curtis met her gaze and gave her a chance to refute Jonas's claim. She would have if the vibes she was picking up off Jonas weren't infused with just any excuse to go upside the man's head. Did they know each other? Was something going on between the two men that she wasn't aware of? She decided the best thing to do for now was to put as much distance between the two men as possible before they came to blows. Based on their expressions, a fight wasn't far off. The friction between them appeared that intense.

When she didn't say anything Curtis turned his attention back to Jonas. The looked that passed between them verified what she'd assumed earlier. They did know each other, and there was something going on that she wasn't privy to, but at the moment felt caught in the middle of.

It was Curtis who finally broke the silence. "Then maybe I should back off."

"Yes, I would highly suggest that you do," Jonas said in what sounded like a low growl. "Now if you will excuse us."

And then he grasped her arm beneath the elbow and leaned close and whispered in her ear in that same low growl, "We need to talk."

She narrowed her eyes at him, and when Curtis walked off, leaving them alone on the patio, she snatched her arm back from Jonas and swirled to face him. "We most certainly do. I want to know what that was about."

Jonas stood staring at Nikki, not sure himself just what that was about. Never in his thirty-three years had he stood before a man and claimed a woman was with him. But a few minutes ago, he had done just that.

"Jonas?"

He drew in a deep breath and said the first thing that came to his mind. "I don't like him."

She frowned. "And you not liking him affects me... how? I believe he stated he wanted to show *me* a good time, not you."

His features suddenly hardened again and he leveled his gaze at her. "He's not getting near you, dammit."

She placed her hands on her hips. "Says who?" she snapped.

"Says me," he snapped back, advancing on her.

She didn't have the good mind to back up and his body pressed against hers. She felt crowded and it was at that moment her temper exploded. "And who the hell are you supposed to be? You're someone I slept with one time. And that's your famous motto—'one and done'—isn't it? Or have you forgotten? In case you have, then let me remind you. One and done, Jonas. And that one time doesn't give you any rights and *you* of all men wouldn't want them if it did. So what in God's name is your problem?"

He rubbed his hand down his face, inwardly acknowledging that he honestly didn't know what his problem was. The only thing he knew was that he wanted her again. Here. Right now. "You, Nikki Cartwright, seem to be my problem," he said in a low steely tone, seconds before grabbing her around the waist, lowering his head and sinking his mouth down on hers.

Chapter 12

Nikki saw it coming and had intended to resist. But all it took was for Jonas to take her mouth with a hunger that sent shivers all through her. Without letting up on her mouth, he drew her closer into the fit of his body, into the juncture of his thighs and right smack into the heat of the hard erection pressing against her.

His hands were no longer on her waist but had moved to her backside as his fingers skimmed sensuous designs all over her bottom while pressing her closer still. She released a tiny whimper from deep in her throat when his tongue seemed to plunge deeper.

Needing to touch him with the same degree of fervor, she placed the palms of her hands at the back of his neck and pulled him closer, locking her mouth even more to his. The silky, soft feel of his hair flowing her over hands as their mouths mated sent intense heat flaring through every part of her body.

Jonas had a way of making her feel both feminine and wantonly wicked at the same time, and there was nothing she could do but slide deeper into his embrace as he continued his sensual assault on her mouth. He was also assaulting her senses, battering them until he had her entire body trembling.

Then suddenly, she felt her legs moving, noted in the hazy part of her mind that he was walking her backward as the cool night air ruffled her curls. She wasn't sure just where he was luring her, but knew as long as he continued to plunder her mouth this way, she was game.

She heard the sound of a glass door sliding open and when he pulled her inside, she pulled her mouth away from his to glance around while drawing in several deep breaths. They were in a small room Ideas of Steele had reserved to store their equipment and supplies for the party.

Before she could say anything, reclaim her senses, he leaned forward and began brushing heated kisses around the corners of her lips. At that moment the only thing she wanted to reclaim was how he was making her feel. She didn't want to do anything but feel his warm breath against the contours of her mouth.

"I want you again, Nikki," he whispered softly before tracing the tip of his tongue along a path down the side of her ear. "I want you so damn bad. I'm going to burst out of my zipper if I don't have you."

Her heart began racing at his words, at the thought that he wanted her that much. But there was something she couldn't let go of and that was why they'd been at odds with each other over the past couple of days. He thought the worst of her. He thought she was someone capable of sharing brothers. And that was unacceptable to her.

She pushed back out of his arms. "I think we need to return to the party. Who knows? Mercury might have surprised us both and arrived in town and is there waiting for me."

He didn't say anything for a second, and then he reached out and took her hand in his, gently held it in his larger one. He stared down at her and met her gaze. "I told you I was sorry about that. It was miscommunication that I acted on without thinking. Don't ask me why I did it, but I did. I acted hastily and I regret it. Deep down I know your character is nothing but wholesome, above reproach."

He paused a moment, released her hand to rub the back of his neck and then said, "And what you said that day is probably true. I'm such a jaded ass that I overlook the decency in others at times. Again, I'm sorry."

"I didn't call you a jaded *ass*."

He chuckled. "No, actually you accused me of sleazy behavior and in my book it practically means the same thing." He got quiet and his expression became serious. "So, will you forgive me?"

She studied his features for a moment. "Will it matter to you if I do or don't?"

He stared at her, as if his gaze was touching every inch of her features, and she could barely breathe under the intensity. Then he finally said, "Yes, it will matter. I like you."

Nikki could only shake her head. Did he actually like her or like sleeping with her? They'd only done so once, but he wanted them to do so again. Tonight. And unfortunately, she wanted to make love with him again as well.

There was just something about the feel of being in his arms, having him planted deep inside of her, intimately connected to her, that made her insides quiver just remembering how it was between them. And it was a way she wanted to be with him again. But what about that "one and done" policy he was known for? Taking her again would be breaking one of his rules. She shrugged. He would be breaking it, not her. The thought of being his "exception" was sending spikes of pleasure through her and making her feel wild and reckless.

"I'm waiting for you to say that you accept my apology and that you like me too, Nikki."

She stared up at him and saw he was serious. There were sober lines etched under his eyes, slashed across his face, and she was tempted to smooth them away with her fingers. Instead, feeling bold, she leaned up on tiptoe and used the tip of her tongue to erase the lines.

Moments later she whispered against his lips, "I accept your apology and I do like you."

And then she went back to licking his sober lines away. Unable to stay mobile under her ministrations, he reached up and began running his fingers through the mass of curls on her head. The feel of his hands in her hair sent her pulse escalating.

And then when her tongue got inches from his mouth, licked his lips from corner to corner, he steadied her head to look at him and whispered, "You're welcome to come inside for a visit."

She did, easing her tongue into his mouth and that's when he crushed her to him and took over the kiss.

He could kiss her forever, Jonas thought as he plundered Nikki's mouth. This was heaven. At least it felt like it anyway. Like he'd told her, he wanted her and he wanted her bad. He wanted to suck on her breasts, lick them all over. Lick her all over. Taste her honeyed warmth again, a taste he hadn't been able to get over.

And then he wanted to make love to her, pump inside of her while her inner muscles clamped down on him. Pulled everything out of him. But he wasn't sure they had time to do all that now. If not now, definitely later. At this moment he would gladly get what he could.

All those thoughts made him slowly pull back from their kiss to look down at her. "Rick is handling things so don't worry about us being missing in action."

"You sure?"

He smiled. "Well, Curtis might miss you, but I won't be missed, trust me."

She chuckled against his lips. "You keep it up and I'm going to start thinking that you're jealous."

He knew she was teasing, but little did she know she had hit pretty close to home. He had gotten jealous. It wouldn't have taken much for him to rip Rhinestone in two. Instead of commenting on what she'd said, he reached out and took her hand in his. He leaned in and murmured against her lips. "Come here, I know just where I want to take you."

He'd said that literally and every cell in his body was ready, invigorated, fully charged. He pressed her hand lightly as he led her around a crate of boxes toward the east side of the room where another set of doors led to a private balcony.

They didn't have a whole lot of time, but he planned to relish to the fullest what they had.

Nikki drew in a deep breath the moment the cool air hit her in the face and shivers ran through her body. Jonas was standing directly behind her and she could feel his heat, his hard erection pressing against her backside. He reached his arms around her and held her around the waist.

"Look up at the stars, baby, and pretend it's just me and you out here in the universe," he whispered. "We are going to make the most of it with a very satisfying, mind-blowing quickie."

She glanced up at the sky. It was clear, with a full moon and twinkling stars. In a few days they would be up there in the sky, flying around in *Velocity*. The thought of them making love while up there sent ripples through her. She knew that she and Jonas would give new meaning to the mile-high club.

"I like this," he murmured close to her ear while his hand moved from her waist to cup her backside. "I like how you twist and bend it while stooping down taking pictures."

His touch felt good and anticipation ran through her when he slowly began easing her pants down her legs, followed by her thong. She stepped out of her shoes and glanced over her shoulder when she saw he had taken off his jacket and tossed it on a nearby bench. The sound of a packet being ripped open let her know he was putting on a condom. She heard the moment he unzipped his pants, and then she felt the long, hard heat of him touching the cheeks of that backside he said he liked so much.

"I love making out with you this way. The feel of being connected to you like this."

Nikki didn't think any man could arouse her the way Jonas did. With both his words and his actions. He liked to talk while seducing a woman and she liked hearing what he had to say. His words were blatant, erotic and usually provided an image that would take her breath away.

"Now for your blouse. We need to take it off as well."

She lifted a brow and under the moonlight she saw him smile. "I locked the door, baby, and this is a private balcony. Nobody is out here but you and me and what you see overhead."

"But you said it would be a quickie."

He took a step toward her, reached out and traced a path along the lacy hem of her blouse. "After the other night you should know that my quickies are also thorough."

He began unbuttoning her blouse as he held her gaze. "Besides, I don't care how quick I intend to be. There's no way I can penetrate you without tasting you all over first."

With the last button undone, her blouse fell open to reveal a black lacy bra. And with a flick of his wrist to the front clasp, the bra came undone and her twin breasts poured forth. "You won't need this for a while," he said, peeling the straps from her shoulders and easing them down her arms, before tossing the bra on the bench to join his jacket and the rest of her things he'd picked up and placed there.

She stood before him totally naked and she hoped everything he said was true. First, that with Rick in charge they wouldn't be missed at the party and secondly, that this was a private balcony.

"Do you know just how beautiful you are?"

She met his gaze and the awe in the depth of his green eyes—eyes that roamed up and down and zeroed in on certain body parts—made her breath catch in her throat.

That night they'd spent together he'd told her a number of times he thought she was beautiful. She had taken his words as those men would typically say to the women they sleep with. But there was a look in Jonas's eyes that made her think that perhaps he really thought so and he wasn't just feeding her a line.

Nikki knew she wasn't bad-looking, but she was far from a gorgeous babe. And she definitely wasn't the sleek and sophisticated type of woman Jonas's name was usually associated with. He probably just found the novelty of her amusing. Yes, that had to be it.

That thought didn't bother her. Things were what they were, and just as long as she kept on a straight head and did not put any more stock into this short, meaningless and oh, so brief affair—if she dared to call it that—then she would be okay.

Whatever other thoughts she wanted to dwell on suddenly flew from her mind when his tongue snaked out and licked around the areola before it wrapped around a nipple, slowly drawing it into his mouth. She could feel the aroused nub swell even more in his mouth. She closed her eyes and felt her inner muscles clench, and she tightened her thighs together to stop the ache starting to build there.

"Not so fast, baby," he said, reaching out and sliding his hand up her thighs to her center. "I want to feel how wet I can make you get."

She recalled how he would intentionally get her wet just to taste her. She had found out that oral sex was something he definitely enjoyed, and by the time he'd finished with her, she had enjoyed it as well.

She moaned the minute his fingers slid inside of her, moved around and plunged deeper as if seeking her moist heat. He touched her clit and began stroking it with his fingertips. Without missing a beat with his fingers, he released one breast and went to the other, giving it the same torment and pushing her even deeper into an aroused state.

He placed her back against the rail as he released her and she didn't open her eyes. She didn't have to. She knew he had lowered to his knees in front of her to make good on what he'd said he intended to do. And when she felt the tip of his hot tongue slide inside of her, locking on to the clit his fingers had tortured earlier, she couldn't stop the whimper that escaped her lips.

She wondered how a man's tongue could go so deep inside a woman. How did it know just what spots to hit to make her moan, whimper and groan?

He released her, leaned back on his haunches and held her gaze. "You like that?"

She drew in a deep breath, not once, but twice before she could answer. "Yes, and I see that you do, too."

He nodded slowly while he licked his lips. "Yes, but just with you." And before she could decide whether he was telling the truth or not, he grabbed hold her of thighs once again, leaned forward and plunged his tongue back into her depths.

She screamed when he began making circular motions with his tongue that had her grabbing his head to hold him there. Right there. How could he make the tip of his tongue feel so hot and find all her erotic places? Her G-spot was definitely taking a licking and then some.

And then suddenly, he did something with his tongue when it caught hold of her clit, wiggled in such a way that made her scream. Luckily the sound was muffled by the noise from the party. She clutched his head tighter to her and he clenched her thighs, locking his mouth to her as a way to let her know he didn't plan on going anyplace.

And only when the last orgasmic spasm flowed from her body did he unlock his mouth from her. She was still whimpering uncontrollably when he gathered her up into his arms and carried her over to the chaise longue. She kept her eyes closed, listening to his erratic breathing.

When she heard him removing his clothes, she drew in enough strength to open one eye and saw him moving toward her like she was his prey. Her gaze latched on to his aroused shaft embedded in a thatch of dark hair. It was so thick, so hard and so big the thought that he was about to use it on her sent sensuous shivers racing through her. She wasn't worried about not being able to fit it in, since she'd done it before. But then she had been pretty sore the next day. Um, maybe now was not the time to—

Before she could finish that thought, he reached out and effortlessly lifted her off the lounger. "Wrap your legs around me," he said in a deep, husky voice. As if he'd spoken to her body and her body alone, it complied and her legs wrapped themselves around him, crossing her ankles at his back.

"Mmm, I like your scent," he said, nuzzling her neck before licking it, then moving from the base of her throat up toward her chin.

"And I like yours," she responded, throwing her head back to give him better access to her neck and throat. This had to be the longest quickie on record. But she had no complaints, especially when she was on such a pleasurable receiving end. She would have to do something extra special to him the next time, and for some reason she had a feeling there would be a next time, at least until she was no longer a novelty.

She felt him spreading her thighs and when he eased the head of his manhood inside of her she couldn't help but moan. "Mmm, we fit perfectly," he said when he grabbed a hold of her buttocks and gripped them tight, pressing them closer into the curve of him.

She was convinced the head of his engorged penis had worked its way right smack into her womb. "What's next?" she asked, like there could be any other ending to what they were doing.

He smiled and she thought he looked so doggone handsome, the way his lips tilted at the corners, and the way that mass of wavy hair on his head made him look wild and untamed. "Now, I'll let your body know who I am."

She chuckled as she tightened her legs around him when he began walking. "I think you did that the last time. I could barely walk the next day."

A huge smile touched his lips as if he was pleased to hear that. She was tempted to pop him upside the head. But injuring him in any way was not at the top of her list. She needed him to finish this. She desperately needed him to finish this.

"Let's sit a spell," he said, easing down on the padded bench.

Sit? She raised a brow. Hadn't he planned to take her against a wall or something? Evidently not as he eased down on the bench, their bodies still connected and facing each other.

"Mmm, now I can look at you," he said, staring into her face. "I want to see you come."

"Do you?"

"Hell, yeah. And I want to see what I can do to you to get you prepared."

No sooner had he finished his sentence, his hands began rubbing her all over, starting at her thighs and then lifting her legs to move down her calves.

He unwrapped her legs from around his back and lifted them high on his shoulders. And their bodies remained connected during the entire process. "How did you know my legs could get raised so high?"

He shifted a little to spread his legs as she sat straddling his lap. "Umm, I figured as much when I saw how you moved around snapping pictures. Anyone who moved the way you did has to have agility down to a science. And you verified my assumptions the last time we made love."

She didn't have to ask how she'd done that. It was during one of those positions he'd sprung on her. She had almost flexed her body into a bow to make sure he didn't miss a thing.

Jonas intruded on her thoughts when he began massaging her legs, kneading her knees and stroking her calves. "You're tense," he said softly. "Relax."

Nikki looked at him. She thought she was relaxed. Maybe he'd gotten her eagerness mixed up with tension. "I'm fine," she said, when she really wasn't.

She was straddling his lap with her legs high on his shoulders while their bodies were connected...and she meant *connected*. If anyone were to see them now they would assume they were glued together, joined at the hips, thighs and definitely the reproductive organs.

"Wiggle a little bit closer."

She didn't think such a thing was possible, considering how close they were already. But she did so, which elevated her legs at a higher angle. "Oh." She felt it. Elevating her legs made her pelvis tilt in a way that stimulated her G-spot. She felt it, all the way to her toes. The sensations had her slanting her bottom for another sensual hit.

"Okay, let's not get carried away, Nikki."

She met his gaze and giggled. "I like you, Jonas."

He threw his head back and laughed. "You would now. But we've wasted enough time. I want to be looking in your face when you scream my name."

And without further ado, he began moving, lifting his hips off the bench as he began thrusting into her, holding her hips in place for every deep, concentrated stroke. She watched him the same way he watched her and saw the intensity in his features as he made love her, increasing the pace with hurried precision, going deeper and deeper, faster and faster with piston speed.

She screamed again when it became too much, the pleasure overtaking her, exploding inside of her and sending her entire body in a tailspin. And he didn't take his eyes off her. She held his gaze and saw when it got to be too much for him as well as he bucked, once, twice and a third time, gripping her thighs tight, holding her body in place as he exploded inside of her.

He ground his hips against hers as a groan was ripped from his throat, but he kept thrusting and she came a second time, calling his name as he continued to rapidly stroke her pulsing flesh. And the erotic waves finally washed over her, cutting her loose from such an intense ride of pleasure. She leaned in and wrapped her arms around him while fighting to regain her breath.

"You are beautiful when you come," he whispered while gently stroking her back.

At that moment she didn't care if he was lying and all he'd seen was an ugly face. On two different occasions he had surpassed all her expectations in the bedroom. He'd proved the real thing was a heck of a lot better than fantasy, but mostly that maybe her head knew what it was talking about when it would tell her to enjoy today and put away the foolish ideas of yesterday.

"If we continue to stay connected like this, I'll be tempted to go another round," he whispered in her ear. The heat of his breath sent blood rushing through her veins.

Nikki knew he was telling the truth. The man had the stamina of a bull. Like the one tattooed on his stomach. She was a living witness to how many orgasms he could get and give in one night. She shifted and noted he was still hard, probably hadn't gone down. She looked at how her legs were hoisted up high on his shoulders and knew if she was going to get them down she needed his help. After all, he had helped get them up there.

"Will you help get my legs down?"

He smiled and she knew she'd made a big mistake. "Sure you want to go back to the party? Our contribution to tonight's affair is over by now."

He shifted positions a little and she felt just how hard he still was. "We need to go back," she said, not using too much of a convincing tone. But then how could she when he was still buried deep inside of her to the hilt and she was feeling him growing bigger and bigger. Her insides were already weeping in joy.

"No, we don't." And then he leaned forward and took her mouth and the only thing she could think of at that moment was that she hoped the noise from the party continued to drown out her screams.

Chapter 13

"So where were you last night, Jonas? I looked around the party and didn't see you anywhere."

Jonas paused in his packing to glance over at Gannon. "I was there, Gan. The only time I was missing was when I had to step out a few minutes for a bit of fresh air."

There was no need to tell his brother that air wasn't the only thing he'd left the party for. And it hadn't been for a few minutes. He'd been missing in action for a little more than an hour. After convincing Nikki to go one more round for the road, he had helped her redress before sending her back to the party ahead of him. He had remained behind to get his bearings and screw his head back on straight. He'd done neither. What he'd done was to remain on that padded bench, stretched out naked as a jaybird while staring up at the sky and remembering every vivid detail of their supposed "quickie."

He had closed his eyes at the memory of how good it had felt being inside of her, how her features took on a whole other look right before an orgasm hit her. He'd never seen anything so gorgeous in his life. Her gaze had held his, and his senses had almost gone on overload at the pleasure he'd seen radiating from her. All the while her inner muscles had clenched him, demanded from him something he'd never given any woman.

And that's when he'd come, exploding all over the place inside of her. Their union had been so explosive, so damn amazing, just thinking about it now had shivers running all through his body. When had mating with a woman done that to him? He should have been prepared for the strength of their lovemaking from the last time, but when it hit him again—that overpowering force that had practically transported him into another place and time—his mind, body and soul had been taken for one hell of a ride. It'd been one damn sexual transportation that had taken him to a whole new hemisphere, maybe another universe.

When he had returned to the party a while later, he hadn't had to worry about being missed. The place was packed. People were everywhere, wall-to-wall, with more trying to get in. He had looked around, but Nikki was nowhere to be found. He would have left the party in search of her if it hadn't been for Mr. Fulton, who'd wanted to talk his ear off.

By the time he'd been able to get rid of the man— who'd had one drink too many and was more than happy with how things had turned out—it was past three in the morning, and too late to go knocking on

Nikki's door. He figured she had to be as drained as he was. Instead he had gone to his own room, stripped naked for the second time that night and fallen in bed with Nikki's scent still clinging to him. Not surprisingly, he had been awakened by a phone call from Gannon, who'd reminded him he had a flight to L.A. that morning. For once he had appreciated his brother's call. Otherwise, he probably would have missed his flight.

"Jonas?"

He blinked when Gannon snapped his fingers in front of his face. He glared at his brother. "What?"

"Damn, man, where were you just now? I was talking to you and you zoned out like you were in another world and you had this downright stupid look on your face."

Jonas frowned as he zipped up his luggage. "You're imagining things." He checked his watch. "Look, I got to go. Thanks for coming and hanging out with me a few days on the Strip."

Gannon chuckled. "The visits to the Doll House and that brothel were worth the trip. Besides, other than those two days before the party, we really didn't spend time together."

Jonas nodded. And only because those were the two days he had been trying to avoid Nikki. "Yeah, but we had fun."

Gannon would be returning to Phoenix later that day. Jonas would be catching a plane to L.A. in time to board the *Velocity*. That's where he and Nikki would be meeting up again. She had an earlier flight, he knew, since she had a meeting with some Hollywood producer about a possible freelancing gig.

He couldn't wait to see her again. There was no reason to ask why. Didn't matter. The woman was so in his system. And what they'd shared last night out on that balcony beneath the moon and the stars was nothing short of spectacular.

He reached out to grab handfuls of his hair to bind it into a ponytail. He had decided at eighteen, much to his mother's dismay, that he would not let another barber do anything more than give him a slight trim. It hadn't mattered that his brothers had teased him mercilessly by calling him Samson. They still did on occasion.

"Have fun while traveling the globe, Jonas."

His thoughts went to Nikki, and he couldn't help but smile. "I'm going to try. What time does your plane take off?"

"Around two. I'm going back to the Doll House to hang out with Quinton. He's quite a character."

Jonas rolled his eyes. Yeah, that wasn't all Quinton Hinton was. A damn bad influence topped the list. Gannon was a grown-ass man, but still, he couldn't help warning his brother. "Don't get into any trouble, Gan."

He didn't particularly like the smile on his brother's face when he responded, "Trust me, I won't."

Nikki walked into the cabin she'd been assigned, still in a daze. She had read everything Jonas had given her on the *Velocity,* but never in her wildest dream had she seen anything so spectacular, magnificent and brilliant. It was as if she was on board the starship *Enterprise* for a taping of *Star Trek.* Everything she saw was not just state-of-the-art; it had to be part of the future.

Even this cabin, for instance, with an octagonal window that was right over the bed, giving her a sky view anytime she wanted it. There wasn't a lot of space, but it was used efficiently, right down to the bed that conformed to the person's size and weight. She'd heard the mattress was comprised of special fibers blended together that guaranteed a perfect sleep each and every time. Good, because she needed a good rest, she thought, yawning. She was still tired from last night.

She couldn't recall what happened without thinking about Jonas. The man was screwing up her head big-time, and her heart didn't stand a chance of getting any talking points into the mix. Each time her heart tried reminding her that Jonas was not her Mr. Right, her head would counter, *Maybe not, but he's definitely a hot and tantalizing Mr. Wrong.*

Deciding she needed sleep more than anything, she was glad the aircraft wouldn't be taking off for another three hours and that she wasn't due to make an appearance until the dinner meeting in another five.

Most of the other people who were on board—who'd been just as fascinated as she about the airship—were still walking around in awe. She had left the group to escape to her cabin the first chance she got. She knew Jonas was scheduled to be on board in a couple of hours, and she needed to pull herself together before seeing him again.

Although she didn't want to listen to her heart at the moment, she knew things couldn't continue like this. Did she really want to become some man's booty girl, a woman he could go to and get laid whenever he wanted? Granted, there was always something in it for her, but still. Didn't she want more? Besides, booty girls weren't the kind men wanted for wives.

And that's the point, Nikki, her head was saying.

When are you going to accept that most men don't want wives? If they did they would be knocking down your door. You're everything any man would want, but that never put you at the top of their list, so chill. Have fun. Stop looking for Mr. Right because he's not out there. Be smart and take what you can get. You don't need a degree in psychology to know most men have issues that you wouldn't want to be bothered with anyway, so why are you so stuck in that forever-after mind-set? Live today and let tomorrow take care of itself.

Nikki drew in a deep breath and placed her hands to her ears. She didn't want to listen to either her head or her heart right now. All she really wanted was more sleep and she was determined to get it.

Jonas glanced at his watch. Where was Nikki? Granted the dinner meeting didn't start for another ten minutes, but he wanted to see her now. He'd made it to the L.A. airport just in time to catch the shuttle that took him over to the gate were the *Velocity* had been docked. Already the media were on it and the place had been jam-packed. It was obvious everyone was in awe of the huge zeppelin that Fulton intended to be the first of many. But first, he had to make sure the *Velocity* was well-received, and it seemed from how things were going so far, it was.

Fulton himself was hosting this dinner meeting, personally welcoming everyone on board. There was no doubt he would wine and dine the media for positive news coverage and already Jonas could tell the man had them eating out of his hands.

Jonas glanced around the room, fought the urge to check his watch again and frowned when he met Curtis

Rhinestone's gaze. He didn't trust him one bit. He had a feeling that although he'd managed to get Nikki away from the man last night, Rhinestone would still try and sniff behind her today, and if the bastard thought for one minute that Jonas would let him, then he had another think coming.

Getting agitated just thinking about it, he decided to move around the room, stretch his legs and appreciate the view. Unlike the others, this wasn't his first time aboard the airship, although this would be the first time he'd been in flight and so far it was smooth flying. He hadn't felt any turbulence, which was one of the *Velocity*'s strong points he would market. Because of the airship's structure it could easily hold its own, even in the most unruly of winds.

The last time he'd been on the *Velocity* had simply been an exclusive tour to see just what sort of marketing scheme he was getting himself into. Then, like now, he'd been truly amazed. There was no doubt in his mind that the *Velocity* would be a huge success. Already the naysayers were questioning the ship's safety and performance but he was certain by the end of this voyage everyone would see just what a remarkable airship this was. That was one of the reasons this trip was so important.

"I was wondering when you were going to get here, Nikki."

He turned at the sound of Curtis's voice and immediately felt his blood boil when Nikki entered the room and Rhinestone got all up in her face. Jonas was tempted to cross the room and smash the man's face in just for the hell of it, but he figured for now he needed to keep his cool. Working for Fulton was an opportunity of a lifetime and he wouldn't jeopardize it with drama. And what was pissing him off more than anything was that Rhinestone knew it.

He took a sip of his tonic water and studied Nikki. Even wearing her signature jeans and shirt she looked beautiful and he absolutely loved the soft-looking curls crowning her face. She had a camera in her hand, ready for business. But all he could think about at that moment was her, naked, straddling him while he thrust in and out of her, making out with her in a way he'd never made out with another women. Not with the same degree of passion, greed or urgency.

He suddenly felt a tingling in his fingers when he remembered them inside of her, stoking her heat, preparing her for his entry. Remembered how when he'd made it in he'd whispered naughty words to her, words that had made her blush while she had creamed some more. The warmth of her skin—whether it had been when their thighs had connected or when her legs had rested high on his shoulders—had wrapped him in a cocoon of sensuality he'd never felt before. She had done more than touch his body last night. She had somehow touched his soul.

Hell, how had that happened?

Had it occurred during those two days he'd tried to avoid her, only to go bonkers when he'd seen her again? Or had it been when they'd made out that night when she'd arrived in Vegas, right on the floor in his suite? For some reason he believed it had been that time when he'd kissed her, and then tried avoiding her for eighteen months. During that time he'd tried to convince himself she was just a woman and he had them anytime he wanted and whenever he wanted. What he hadn't counted on was her being different from all the others. He hadn't thought any woman capable of drawing out emotions in him, some of which he hadn't known he was capable of having. Like the need to do bodily harm to anyone who looked at her for too long.

Rhinestone glanced over his way with a smirk on his face. Jonas forced back the anger that tried rising to the top, well aware of the game the man intended to play. And if he thought he would play that game with Nikki then he was sorely mistaken.

Jonas inhaled deeply He refused to stand on the sidelines and let Curtis, or any man, make a move on Nikki. Curtis knew how he operated and until he made a public claim for a woman, the man wouldn't be backing off. And anyone who knew Jonas knew his hard and steadfast rule against ever doing such a thing. There were too many women out there to ever lay claim to just one.

He tried ignoring Rhinestone standing so close to Nikki. That resolve lasted all but two seconds. He placed his glass on the tray of a passing waiter and headed across the room after deciding it was time to break his own rule yet again.

Chapter 14

Nikki did the polite thing and nodded a few times while Curtis and another reporter conversed about how fascinated they were with the *Velocity*. She was surprised at the way Curtis had greeted her, especially after the obvious tension between him and Jonas last night.

She scanned the room, deliberately not allowing her gaze to wander where Jonas was standing. She'd seen him the moment she'd arrived and her heart had skipped a beat when he'd turned and their gazes had connected.

He was wearing his hair back in a ponytail and anytime he did so it only highlighted the angular lines of his face and showed a handsomeness that would take any woman's breath away. Dressed casually in a pair of jeans and a shirt, he was the epitome of masculine perfection.

She'd seen his frown when Curtis had stopped her. It was obvious he didn't like it. She really shouldn't care what he liked or didn't like because no matter how many times they came together, it was just for sex. He knew it as well as she.

"So what are your plans when we reach Beijing?" Curtis asked her, pulling her back into the conversation. "Surely you won't be expected to work while we're docked."

She opened her mouth to respond when a shadow crossed her path just seconds before a pair of lips brushed across hers in a kiss. Then a deep, masculine voice said, "Hello, sweetheart. I've been waiting for you and as usual, you were worth the wait."

For the hell of it, Jonas decided to brush a second kiss across her lips just to wipe the shocked look off her face. He stood by her side and wrapped his arms around her waist, ignoring the tension he felt flowing through her. He then turned to the two men and reached out for handshakes. "Rhinestone. Loggins. Good seeing you guys again. I hope you're enjoying yourselves."

He inwardly smiled at the way Rhinestone was recovering from a dropped jaw. The man was just as shocked as Nikki. He and Rhinestone weren't just fraternity brothers, they'd pledged on the same line. Kissing Nikki in front of everyone was a public claim to show their relationship was more than just casual. For Curtis to trespass on a fellow frat brother was a social taboo, a violation of the code of honor, something he wouldn't do.

"So how long have the two of you been involved?" Rhinestone asked, taking a sip of his drink and holding Jonas's gaze.

Jonas was quick with a response, which was a question of his own. "Why do you want to know?"

"Curious."

He was tempted to tell Rhinestone just what he could do with his curiosity, but instead said, "Long enough. Now if you gentlemen will excuse us, I think Fulton is ready for dinner to begin."

Taking Nikki's arm beneath the elbow, he led her to one of the tables in the room. He sensed her anger and knew she was holding her peace longer than he'd expected. Eventually she would let him have it but wouldn't do it here.

He leaned closer, considered her a moment and then asked, "You okay?"

She inclined her head and the gaze staring at him was filled with fury. "What do you think?"

He forced his lips to form a thin smile. "I don't know. That's why I asked. And no, I'm not trying to be a smart-ass."

"Then what are you trying to be?" she asked as they sat down at a table set for two. He'd deliberately chosen this one for privacy.

When they'd taken their seats, he leaned closer and whispered to her, his breath fanning the side of her face, "What I *intend* to be is the only man who's going to pleasure you on this air voyage."

Less than six hours later Nikki walked down the corridor that led to her hotel room. The *Velocity* had docked at the Beijing Airport without any problems.

Everything at the dinner party had gone well. Fulton had welcomed everyone on board and introduced his twelve flight attendants—males and females who looked like they had stepped off the covers of *GQ* and *Cosmo*. But she had to hand it to them, they had been true professionals and their customer service skills had been superb.

The meal they were served at dinner would rival that at any five-star restaurant. It was hard to believe they had dined while flying more than forty thousand feet in the air. Except for during takeoff and landing, they had been free to roam about the airship to enjoy the shopping boutiques, casino, library, game room and restaurant.

Jonas hadn't left her side the entire evening, clinging on to her like a grape to a vine. But she'd refused to indulge in private conversation with him. She ignored his air of possession whenever they conversed with others and got annoyed at how easily he would slide his arms around her waist and bring her closer to his side whenever another male got near, becoming territorial. When she hadn't been able to stand it anymore, she had feigned a migraine and gone to her cabin. He had offered to go with her to make sure she was okay, but she had turned down his offer and made it quite clear that she wanted to be alone. He'd called later to check on her, but when she answered the phone she had told him they had nothing to say to each other.

Reservations had been made for each passenger at several hotels in Beijing, where they would remain for three days on their own. She was grateful for that decision since she definitely needed to put distance between her and Jonas, even if only for three days.

As soon as the airship had docked, she had switched groups with another passenger and ridden off in a different limo from the one she'd been assigned. She felt good knowing Jonas had no idea where she was and wouldn't be seeing her again until they returned to the *Velocity* to continue their air voyage to Australia. As far as she was concerned, he could play his little game all by himself.

She rubbed her temple after entering her hotel room and closing the door behind her. What had she done in going along with Jonas's deception that they were involved in an affair? Sleeping with a man twice didn't constitute an affair, and considering his reputation, Jonas of all people knew that. So what if he'd transitioned from one-and-done to twice-is-nice? The only thing he'd accomplished was to gain triumph over Curtis, a man who evidently was his adversary. And he had used her to do it.

She glanced at her watch. It was in the middle of the day in Beijing, but her body was still in the Pacific time zone. She would sleep the day through and then tomorrow she would go out and do some sightseeing. By the time she returned to the *Velocity,* she would be able to handle the likes of Jonas Steele and set the record straight once and for all. They were not involved.

Jonas stared at the smiling flight attendant. "What do you mean Ms. Cartwright departed the *Velocity* a few hours ago?"

The young woman nodded. "Yes, sir. She requested a change in her itinerary and we were able to work something out with another passenger. She was in the first group that departed."

He drew in a deep agitated breath. He should have followed his mind and checked on her although she'd told him she wanted to be left alone. But he'd figured he would let her get some rest and then talk to her later. When she hadn't come out of her cabin for a while, he'd figured she had decided to grab a few more hours of rest, since they were the last group scheduled off the airship.

His gaze went back to the woman. "Then I'd like to know where she's gone since obviously she's no longer in my group and won't be staying at my hotel."

The woman's smile remained in place. "Yes, sir, but we can't divulge that information."

He of all people should know that. A high degree of privacy was one of *Velocity*'s strongest marketing points. He would have to use another approach. "Ms. Cartwright works for me and I need to get a message to her."

He knew before he'd finished talking that the woman wasn't buying it. She was one of the attendants who had worked the dinner meeting last night and had seen how he'd been all over Nikki. No matter what he said, the woman knew their relationship wasn't all business and if he couldn't find his woman then there must be trouble in paradise and she wasn't getting involved.

His woman.

Where had that thought come from? He shook his head. Damn. For the time being Nikki *was* his woman. He had pretty much claimed as much last night in a public display. And hadn't he made it clear to her that he intended to be the only man who would pleasure her on this voyage? Evidently she was still upset about last night and what he needed to do was talk to her as soon as possible. Hopefully, the two of them could reach some sort of an agreement.

"Do you not have her cell phone number, sir?"

"Yes, but I can't reach her." What he wouldn't say was that Nikki wasn't answering her phone.

"Sorry to hear that. Is there anything else, sir?"

He looked down at the woman, seeing she wasn't going to bend. He glanced down at her name tag. "No, Mandy, there's nothing else."

Jonas moved on as his mind began working. He'd always had ways of finding out whatever it was he wanted. One person who would know where Nikki had run off to was Brittany. However, he doubted his sister-in-law would tell him anything. He could turn to Galen to coax the info from his wife, but that would mean spilling his guts as to why he wanted to know. It was one thing to give a handful of strangers the impression he was enamored with a woman, but to give his brothers that same impression was another. He would never live it down.

That meant he would have to go to plan B and he had no qualms doing so. He had seen the way Mandy had ogled Rick last night and Rick's reputation as a ladies' man was just as bad as his. Jonas felt certain Rick could make more strides with Mandy than he had.

Rick owed him a favor and it was time for him to collect.

Nikki shifted in bed to drown out the insistent knocking at her hotel room door. Why was the cleaning service bothering her? Hadn't they seen the do-not-disturb sign on her door? "Go away," she called out before burying her head beneath her pillow.

When the knocking continued, she threw back the bed covers and stormed out of the bedroom to the door, pausing only to grab her robe off a chair. Customer service would definitely hear about this. She had wanted to rest for at least twelve hours. Jet lag was a bitch.

Nikki stopped halfway to the door when it opened. She crossed her arms over her chest, ready to take the person to task for disturbing her sleep. Her mouth dropped open when the person who walked across the threshold was not someone from housekeeping.

It was Jonas.

Chapter 15

"What are you doing here?"

After closing the door behind him, Jonas stood there, almost dazed, staring at her and thinking that with her curls tossed all over her head, bare feet and in a short robe showing a luscious pair of thighs, Nikki looked absolutely breathtaking.

She also looked absolutely mad. Furious was more like it.

"I asked what you're doing here, and what gives you the right to just come into my hotel room?"

He tossed his jacket on a chair. "I'm here to spend time with you. Someone from housekeeping heard me banging on your door, was fearful I'd wake up the whole floor, so she unlocked your door for me."

Nikki glared at him. "Wrong move on her part. I'm going to make sure she doesn't have a job much longer."

"Boy, you're mean."

"And you're leaving. Goodbye."

He shook his head and pushed his hair back from his face. He hadn't had time to bind it back after finding out Nikki's whereabouts. It hadn't taken Rick long to discover what hotel she'd gone to, and Jonas had caught the first taxi here. "I'm not leaving, Nikki."

"Fine, then I'll call security," she tossed over her shoulder as she headed for the phone.

"I wouldn't if I were you. Things could get pretty messy. More than likely your actions will generate gossip, fodder for the tabloids. I can see our faces plastered in the papers back home. Should be interesting reading."

She crossed her arms over her chest and stared him down. "You have more to lose than I do, Jonas. So what's it going to be?"

He crossed his arms over his own chest, stood with his legs spread apart and glared right back at her. "I'll tell you what it's going to be. You. Me. We have it out now, Nikki. You're still mad at me for what I did at that dinner party. Why? I thought women preferred knowing a man was interested in them. Last night I did something I've never done before, and that was to claim you as mine in front of everyone. So what's the problem?"

Nikki was convinced he really didn't have a clue. The man was so used to being in control, doing whatever the hell he wanted to do where women were concerned, that he thought *claiming* her was doing her a favor. Well, she had news for him. She didn't want to be claimed. She wanted to be loved.

Yes, yes, it was her heart talking again and she couldn't help it. The truth had hit her full force in the face at dinner. He had pampered her with attention, given her a taste of how things could be between them if they were in love. He hadn't left her side and had touched her easily, sliding his arms around her waist like it had been the most natural thing.

And every time he'd looked at her, although she'd tried to stay mad, her heart would leap in her chest, making her realize that without a doubt she had fallen in love with him. Though she had probably been in love with him for a while, at dinner she had opened her eyes and given in to her heart.

Giving in to her heart was one thing she could not abide. Admitting her love for Jonas had no place in this argument and there was no way he would ever know how she felt. There was no use. The man wasn't capable of loving a woman. That wasn't part of his makeup. He had probably figured out in that player mind of his that kissing her in front of everybody would entitle him to unlimited access to her bed. Well, she had news for him.

"I don't want to have it out with you, Jonas. I just want to be left alone."

"Do you?" he threw back. "I don't think so."

"I don't care what you think."

"Then maybe you should," he said, slowly moving toward her like a hunter who'd targeted his prey.

Nikki drew in a deep breath, convinced the man was mad. He was also sexy as hell. How could he not be when he was unbuttoning his shirt with every step he took? She backed up. "I don't want you, Jonas."

"Then I guess I'm going to have to change your mind about that."

She refused to back up any farther, deciding to stand her ground. She placed her hands on her hips and stared him down. "What is it with you Steeles? Why do you assume you can get any woman you want?"

He shrugged. "I can't speak for my brothers, but as for myself, the only woman I want is you."

She looked up at him. "Why?"

"I can give you a number of reasons. No woman can wear a pair of jeans like you do. Seeing your curvy bottom in them makes me hard each and every time. Then there are those soft curls on your head that frame your face. It's such a beautiful face."

His gaze went to her chest. "And then there're your breasts that fit perfectly in my hands."

His gaze shifted lower to the juncture of her thighs. He smiled. "The only thing I can say about *that* part is that I think I'm addicted to it. I love tasting it, touching it and getting all into it any way I can."

She lifted her chin. "Sounds all sexual to me."

"Probably because I'm a sexual kind of guy. But no matter how much I enjoy it, you're the only woman who has me wanting to come back for more, wishing there was a way I could stay locked inside you forever, make you a permanent taste bud on my tongue."

She knew it had to be a deliberate move on his part because her body was ripening with every word he said. Her panties were getting wet, her nipples felt sensitive against her robe and her lips were tingling. She should be fighting his assault on her senses, but she was getting pulled into a stream of mindless pleasure. The kind she knew he could deliver.

He slowly began advancing upon her again and she still held her ground, feeling the charged energy radiating between them that was breaking down her defenses, playing havoc with her senses one turbulent sensation at a time. She drew in a deep breath and filled her nostrils with his masculine scent and felt intense desire flood her middle.

"Why do you want to fight me, Nikki, when all I want to do is make love to you?"

His words were like ice water being dumped on a heated surface. She took a step back and narrowed her gaze. "You wouldn't know how to make love to a woman if it killed you, Jonas. All you know how to do is have sex with one. There is a difference."

He came to a stop in front of her. "Then show me how to make love. In fact I have a proposition for you. I propose that we enter into a private arrangement where for the rest of our trip on the *Velocity,* we don't have sex, but we make love."

She rolled her eyes. Those words just confirmed what she already knew. He didn't have an idea of what love was if he thought the arrangement he was proposing was possible. "Love isn't anything you can speak into existence. People can only *make* love when they are *in* love."

He reached out, wrapped an arm around her waist, drawing her closer. "In that case, let's pretend we're in love, then. You know that I don't love you and I know that you don't love me, but if it makes you feel better, we can pretend."

A part of Nikki couldn't believe he would suggest such a thing, but then another part of her did believe it. Although his parents were still happily married and he had two brothers who were also in happy marriages, Jonas just didn't get it, mainly because he'd never felt that emotion himself, and she wondered if he ever would. Who knew, maybe if he got a taste of it, he might like it.

She shook her head. Her thoughts were beginning to be just as insane as his, which meant her head was filling up with crazy ideas and ludicrous notions. Men like Jonas didn't fall in love. They didn't even know the meaning of it. But maybe if he were to pretend long enough…

There was that silly thought again. Besides, it wouldn't be any pretense on her part, so what would that do to her heart when he decided he didn't even like the pretend version? But then if she did enter into such a private arrangement with him, it would help her to move on and accept that the man she loved would never love her back.

She hadn't told anyone yet about the job offer she'd gotten from the L.A. producer who'd interviewed her before she boarded the *Velocity*. He'd been so impressed with her portfolio that he had called just minutes before the airship had taken off and made her a job offer as set photographer. The salary he'd offered had almost made her fall out of the bed in her cabin. And since he'd be directing a miniseries that would take three years of filming, it would be steady work for a long while.

The only drawback she'd seen at the time was moving from Phoenix to L.A. for those three years. But now, considering everything, the move to L.A. wouldn't be a drawback but a blessing. If she considered Jonas's offer of a private arrangement, the next two

weeks would be all she would ever have before she left
Phoenix to start a new life on the coast.

Jonas placed his finger beneath her chin so their
gazes could connect. "So, baby, are you game?" he
asked in a low tone, the depths of his green eyes holding hers. "Women are into this love thing more so
than men, so if you want to pretend that you got me all
strung out for you then that's fine. And just so we're
clear, our arrangement ends when the *Velocity* docks
back in L.A."

He moved closer still, so close his thighs were touching hers, and she could feel the hardness of his erection
press against her stomach. And it felt so good resting
there. So hot. So tempting.

"I can see you're hesitant. Maybe I need to give you
something to help you make up your mind," he murmured, lowering his head to lick her lips.

"Something like what?" she asked, feeling her senses
ooze away from her.

"Something like this."

He pushed the robe from her body and quickly removed her short baby-doll nightie as well. Then, as effortlessly as any man could do, he lifted her up off her
feet and stood her naked body on the edge of the couch
with her thighs spread apart.

"Jonas, I think that we—"

"Shh," he whispered, stepping back to remove his
clothes and put on a condom although she knew she was
on the pill. He then moved back to the couch to stand
in front of her. "Bend your knees a little, baby, so I can
ease inside you," he said in a deep husky tone.

She did as he asked and then glanced down to
watch how the head of his engorged penis penetrated

her flesh and slid deep inside of her. It fascinated her that something that large could fit inside of her so perfectly. Reaching out, he grabbed her hips to hold her body steady as he made the journey in. As deep as he could go. Then he reached out to lave her breasts with his tongue, licking all over the areola before sucking a turgid nipple into his mouth.

"You're starting to cream all over me and I like it," he said as he released her nipple. "It's hot and thick. Just the way I like to feel it. Just the way I love to taste it. But for now I want to pump you up. Give you reason to want to pretend we're in love."

And then the lower part of his body began moving as he captured her mouth, mating with it the same way he was mating with her womanly core. She moved to his rhythm as their bodies rocked and rolled, and she met his every thrust. And then he picked up speed and power, beginning to pound into her while he gripped her backside to hold her in place while he went deeper still, as if carving out his place inside of her.

"I can't get enough of you," he growled and she knew what he meant, mainly because she couldn't get enough of him, either. She widened her legs and the moment she did so, her senses spun out of control as he hit her G-spot.

She lifted her legs off the couch to wrap them around his waist as tight as they could get. He deepened the kiss and moved from the sofa to the nearest wall, where he pressed her back against the solid surface and continued to pound into her like the world would be ending tomorrow and he needed every thrust to count.

And they did.

Only with him was her body this sharp, keen, capable of feeling every single sensation he evoked. This was crazy. This was madness. And in the back of her mind she was reminded this was just sex. For him, yes, but not for her. He might be having sex with her, but she was definitely making love to him.

And then her body exploded under his forceful thrusts and she screamed his name as an orgasm ripped solidly into her, almost blinding her. It not only assaulted her body, it beat up on her senses. Whipped them to the point of no return. At that moment nothing mattered but this and how he was making her feel. She ignored that little chat from her heart that she deserved better. Instead she listened to her head. *You can't get any better than this.*

Jonas followed suit, roaring loudly on the heels of a deep masculine growl. He gritted his teeth while the lower half of his body continued to grind into her nonstop. He was pulling everything out of her and was still demanding more. And he was doing it in such a way that she felt every single movement. Never had she felt more connected to any man than right now.

She wrapped her arms around his neck and met his gaze. No words were exchanged between them. None was needed. And then their mouths joined again in a long, sensuous kiss.

Yes, she would agree to the private arrangement that he wanted, and when they returned to Phoenix she would be ready to move on with her life in another city.

It would be far away from the heartbreak she knew awaited her if she were to stay.

Chapter 16

"Okay, I give up," Jonas said, staring at the item on the serving tray that a waiter had just placed in front of them. "What is it?"

Nikki chuckled. "It's the carcass of the duck we had for dinner. The Chinese don't believe in letting anything go to waste so they fried it for us."

He arched his brow. "And we're supposed to eat it?"

"Yes."

He wiped his mouth and tossed his napkin on the table and leaned back in his chair. "I'll pass. I'm full already. What about you?"

She smiled over at him. "I'm full as well. Dinner was wonderful."

He would have to agree with her. The staff at their Beijing hotel had recommended this restaurant, and he had selected items off the menu that he recognized and had gone along with Nikki to try a few dishes he hadn't been familiar with and had enjoyed them as well. But he would draw the line with duck carcass.

Jonas studied Nikki as she sipped her tea, finding it hard to believe they'd spent the last two days together in perfect harmony. At first he had questioned his sanity in suggesting their private arrangement. To pretend to be in love with a woman had to be one of the craziest notions he'd ever come up with. But so far things were working.

He enjoyed watching her sleep and how her curls would fan her face and the soft snoring sounds she would occasionally make. And then in the mornings when she would wake up, he liked how she would smile up at him before reaching out for what had become their good-morning kiss. Of course that kiss would lead to other things.

"So, what will we do today?"

Her question pulled him from his thoughts and he glanced across the table at her. Her eyes were just as bright as her smile. "I'll let you decide today since yesterday's activities were my idea."

"Yeah, and you whined the entire time."

He looked offended. "I did not whine."

She leaned in closer across the table. "You did too, Jonas Steele."

He laughed. "Okay, maybe I did."

It had been his idea for them to climb the Great Wall of China, but halfway up he was ready to go back down. He hadn't known the place would require so much energy—energy he preferred using for other things like making love to her. Even now he was still overwhelmed by the power of what they shared in the bedroom. They were doing things the same way, but he could swear he was beginning to note a difference. A difference he couldn't quite put his finger on.

"In that case, since you're letting it be my decision, I suggest we take a cooking class."

He sat up straight in his chair. "A cooking class?"

She chuckled. "Yes."

He crossed his arms over his chest. "Why would I want to attend a cooking class? I have a woman who comes in twice a week to clean and cook enough food to last me all week. Then there are my weekly Thursday dinners at my parents' home. I don't need to know how to cook."

"I think it will be fun."

"Whatever," he said, taking a sip of his own tea. "I guess I'm game if that's what you really want to do."

Her smile brightened even more. "Yes, that's what I really want to do."

He smiled, enjoying the smile that curved her lips. "Okay. Where's my apron?"

With shopping bags in each hand, Nikki entered her hotel room and used her feet to shut the door behind her. All the passengers would return to the *Velocity* later that day and she had wanted to get some shopping in before the limo arrived to transport her and Jonas to the airport. Their next stop was Sydney, Australia, where they would be spending another three days.

Earlier that morning after making love, she and Jonas had toured a Chinese palaces and Tiananmen Square. Afterward, they'd shared lunch at, of all places, Friday's. Jonas had been tickled to see an American chain restaurant and insisted on going. She had invited him to go shopping with her in the afternoon, but he declined, saying he wanted to return to the hotel for a quick nap.

Nikki glanced at her watch. That had been three hours ago and from the soft hum of his snoring, it seemed he was still at it. Quietly placing her bags on the sofa, she tiptoed out of the sitting area into the bedroom. She leaned in the doorway and stared across the room at the man she loved.

His upper torso, not covered by the bed linens, was bare, as she was certain the rest of him was since he loved sleeping in the nude. She blushed when she recalled how he now had her sleeping in the nude as well, something she had learned was an enjoyable experience. Especially since Jonas had a tendency to wake up during the crazy hours of the night wanting to make love.

Nikki stepped into the room, closer to the bed. With his mass of hair all over the pillow, the man was pure temptation even while asleep. She drew in a deep breath. These would be the only days she would have with him this way, trouble free, filled with fun and excitement, and both beginning and ending with them connected in a way that took her breath away just thinking about it. It always felt good being wrapped in his embrace, held by him, hearing whispered erotic words that could make her come just listening to them.

She was about to move away from the bed when suddenly his hand snaked out and grabbed her around the wrist. She looked down at him and saw his eyes were open and the depth of his green eyes had her holding her breath.

His hold on her hand tightened when he continued

to stare at her. Then he said in a deep husky tone, "I want you, baby. And I want you now."

He pulled her into the bed with him, almost tore off her clothes, and it seemed within seconds after donning a condom he retrieved from the night stand, he was straddling her, easing between her legs, slowly penetrating her, deep and sure.

Gracious! Him inside of her felt so right. Why couldn't he see it? Why couldn't he feel it? Why couldn't he love her as much as she loved him? There were too many whys for her to concentrate on at the moment. Not when he was thrusting inside her so hard the whole bed was shaking.

"Come for me, baby. I want you to cream all over me," he said, breathing the words against her neck.

And she did, calling out to him while lifting her hips to take him in as far as possible. Their days were numbered, but she was determined to collect as many memories as she could.

"Brittany is pregnant?" Jonas asked, not believing what his brother Galen had just told him.

"Yes, and I'm so happy about it I can't stand it."

Jonas nodded, hearing that excitement in his brother's voice. And then he couldn't help but chuckle when he recalled what he'd suggested to his mother a few weeks earlier about hitting Galen and Brittany up for a grandchild. He could just imagine his mother's happiness and excitement as well.

"Have you told Mom yet?" he asked.

"No, we're telling her tonight when we go to the folks' place for dinner."

Jonas would give anything to be there to see the expression on Eden's face when they did. Expecting a grandbaby should definitely keep her busy and out of her single sons' business for a while.

"If you see Nikki, don't mention anything to her. Brittany wants to be the one to tell her. I think she's going to ask Nikki to be our baby's godmother."

Jonas nodded thinking Nikki would make a good choice for godmother. They had spent a lot of time together over the past two weeks, and he had been exposed to a side of her he hadn't seen before. He saw she was generous to a fault, liked to have fun and was loyal to those she considered friends. Like him she was close to her family, and like his, her parents had been married for a long time.

A part of him was trying to forget that tomorrow they would be returning home. At least he would. She mentioned that she had a meeting with someone in L.A. and wouldn't be back in Phoenix until the end of the week.

Jonas knew that everyone traveling on the *Velocity* could say that it had been one hell of a voyage and that they had had the experience of a lifetime. There was no doubt in his mind the reviews written by the media on board would be favorable, and it would be up to his staff to capitalize on the good publicity and roll out the marketing campaign that would guarantee a sellout as soon as *Velocity* took its next voyage.

He couldn't help but think of this one. After Beijing they had traveled to Australia, from there to Dubai and finally to Paris. They had covered four continents in fourteen days. Tomorrow they would leave Paris for L.A.

"Jonas?"

It was then that he recalled his brother's request. "Okay, I won't say anything to Nikki," he answered.

No one knew he and Nikki were involved other than those who saw them together on the airship. But he didn't care if the whole world knew it. The only thing was their affair would be ending soon so sharing the information was a moot point now.

Moments later he ended his call with Galen to walk over to the window and look out. This hadn't been his first visit to Paris and wouldn't be his last. He loved the place, with its elegant architecture, beautiful countryside and majestic castles. Everyone was staying at Chateau d'Esclimont, which was an hour outside of Paris. The place was simply breathtaking and nestled in the Loire Valley. He had discovered Nikki could ride a horse and the two of them had ridden two Thoroughbreds around the countryside. And then later they'd had a picnic near a picturesque lake.

Australia had been just as magnificent. It been somewhat strange knowing it was winter in the States and arriving in Sydney during the heart of their summer. He and Nikki had totally enjoyed themselves, taking a tour of the city and flying over the Great Barrier Reef. Seeing one of the seven wonders of the natural world had been totally captivating, something he would never forget.

And Dubai was certainly a place he would return to. There was nothing like sailing on the Persian Gulf and taking a camel ride across the desert. He couldn't help but smile when he recalled how Nikki had blushed profusely at the sight of camels mating. And then later that night, back in their hotel room, they'd done a little camel-like mating of their own.

He moved away from the window. The time he'd spent with Nikki was something he couldn't forget, either. She had brought something into the last two weeks that he hadn't expected. Namely, the kind of companionship he hadn't expected to find with any woman. She was someone he could talk to about anything, and he definitely enjoyed their conversations. Considering their rocky beginning, he was simply amazed at how well they got along. That didn't mean they agreed on anything, far from it. But they had a very satisfying way of compromising when they did disagree.

He was finding out that pretending to love a woman had its benefits, although he wouldn't want to do that with any other woman. Besides, he couldn't imagine any other woman agreeing to such a deal. But Nikki had. She had agreed to this private arrangement between them, and he didn't regret making it.

The only thing he regretted was that tomorrow things would come to an end. There was no doubt in his mind that he and Nikki would run into each other on occasion, but he would resume his life as he knew it and she would resume hers.

Yesterday he had viewed all the photographs she'd taken and of course he hadn't been disappointed. She had done an excellent job and he couldn't wait for the marketing campaign to move forward.

Once she emailed him all the photographs, her employment with Ideas of Steele would cease. He would pay her for her services and that would be it.

His hands shook when he tried pouring coffee from the pot in the room. After spending two such glorious weeks with Nikki, how was he supposed to get back into the swing of things without her? At that moment, the thought of becoming involved with another woman, going back to his "one and done" rule just didn't have the appeal it had once had.

Even worse, the thought of his manhood sliding between any woman's legs other than Nikki's, or his head being buried between any other woman's thighs, or his mouth mating with any other woman's, was leaving a bad taste in his mouth.

He put down his coffee cup and ran his fingers over his chin, feeling the stubble there. What in the hell was wrong with him? No woman had ever made him feel this way and, dammit, he didn't like it one bit. He needed to get ready to get his groove on once again, be the player he was. There were all those models, socialites and party girls who wanted to share his bed. He was certain any one of them could get him back on the right track, put his mind back in check. And put Nikki way in the back of it.

She'd been fun, enjoyable, but now it was time for them to move on, and they would because when the *Velocity* landed in Los Angeles, their private arrangement as they knew it would be over.

Tears of happiness sprang into Nikki's eyes. "Oh, Britt, that is so wonderful. Congratulations. I am so happy for you and Galen."

And she truly was. She knew Galen and Britt's relationship was solid and they loved each other very much. To Nikki, having a baby, one conceived in love, had to be the most rewarding thing that could happen to a woman.

"I can't wait until you get back. We're going to have to celebrate," Brittany cut into her thoughts and said.

Nikki agreed. "Yes, we will. I'll be back in the States later today, but I've got another meeting with Martin Dunlap before I come back to Phoenix."

"So you are going to take that job in Los Angeles?"

"Yes, I think it will be for the best. I'm at a place in my life where I need to make a change."

She drew in a deep breath. In less than two hours the *Velocity* would be leaving its docking station in Paris to return home. Everyone was on board and accounted for, and Jonas was in a private meeting with Fulton. She knew the man was pleased with how this trial voyage had turned out, and so far all the media coverage had been positive. She'd heard that people were already clamoring to get tickets for the next trip, which was scheduled in two weeks.

"I hate that we're going to be separated again, Nikki."

Nikki hated that, too. She and Brittany had lived across the street from each other while in their early teens, and when Nikki's military dad had received orders to move to another port, Nikki and Brittany had lost touch. They had found each other a year and a half ago when Brittany had come to Phoenix on business. She and Galen had met and the rest was history.

"We'll never be separate, Britt. I'll just be a plane ride away. Besides, now that you've asked me to be the baby's godmother, you'll be seeing me more than you think."

Brittany chuckled. "Yes, and I believe that one day you'll have all those babies of your own that you've always wanted."

Nikki wished that was true but wouldn't be holding her breath for that to happen. "Maybe. But in the meantime, I'll spoil my little goddaughter or godson rotten."

A short while later, after she ended her call with Brittany, Jonas returned to the cabin. After their decision regarding their private arrangement, they had begun sharing a cabin. They'd decided to use his since it had been the larger of the two.

He glanced over at her the moment he entered the room. He must have seen her red eyes, because he crossed the room and pulled her into his arms. "Hey, you okay?"

She nodded and looked up at him. "Yes, I just finished talking to Brittany. She told me about her and Galen's good news. She also told me that you were sworn to secrecy."

He chuckled. "Yes. That kind of news definitely made my parents happy. Galen and Brittany told them last night. I hear my mother is already buying out the baby stores."

Nikki could just imagine. She remembered how her mother had behaved when her brother and sister-in-law presented her parents with their first grandbaby.

Jonas stroking her back felt good. Being in his arms felt good as well. Boy, she was definitely going to miss this. Neither of them had broached the subject of what would happen when the *Velocity* arrived in Los Angeles. They didn't have to. It had been part of the agreement. He would go his way and she would go hers.

Of course their paths would cross in Phoenix from time to time. There was no way around it, and there was always the chance they might work together again. But the intimacy they'd shared would become a thing of the past. Their relationship would move from friends with benefits to just friends.

She pulled out of his arms and looked up at him. "I'm fine. How did things go with Fulton?"

"Great. He had a chance to look at the portfolio you put together and said you did a wonderful job. He told me to tell you that."

"Thanks." Their relationship was changing already. She could feel it. Although they had made love that morning, she had felt him beginning to withdraw. Her heart was breaking inside, but a part of her understood that that's the way things were to be. Nothing lasted forever, even if it was pretend.

Their gazes held and she felt the yearning stir within her as it always did. He had that effect on women. He certainly had that effect on her. But did they have time now? They would be docking in L.A. in less than four hours. There was a part of her that wished time could stand still.

"Nikki, I—"

She reached out and placed her finger to his lips. "I know and it's okay. I had a good time and I hope you did, too."

He nodded. "I did."

He pulled her back to him and lowered his head toward hers. She had gotten her answer. They would make love one last time. This would be their goodbye. And despite everything, she had no regrets.

Chapter 17

Three weeks later

"**Y**ou're awfully quiet tonight, son. Usually you're the life of the party."

Jonas glanced up at his dad, a man whom he highly admired and respected. Over forty years ago Drew Steele had taken his small trucking company and turned it into a million-dollar industry that had routes all over the United States.

Another one of his father's accomplishments was always making time for his six sons, no matter how busy he'd been. And although he and his brothers would moan and groan about his parents' Thursday-night chow-down, where their attendance was expected, deep down they appreciated it as a way to stay connected, no matter how busy their schedules were.

Jonas forced a smile to his lips. "I'm fine. Besides, I decided to take a backseat to Gannon tonight since he seems to have a lot to say."

Drew chuckled. "Yes, I can see that." He paused a moment, then said, "I understand that the four-continent air voyage was a huge success and your company's marketing campaign was instrumental in getting it over the top. Congratulations."

"Thanks." Deep down he felt the credit should go to Nikki. Those photographs she'd taken had helped to introduce the *Velocity* into the market. His social media guru had taken Nikki's pictures and had done a fantastic job in incorporating them in the Ideas of Steele marketing plan.

Nikki.

He gazed down into his glass of wine wondering how she'd been doing. More than once he'd been tempted to pick up the phone to call her and ask. But each time he had talked himself out of doing so. Something was going on with him and at the moment he didn't have a clue as to what. All he knew was that as of yet he hadn't been able to get back into his game. Hell, the thought of kissing another woman had almost made him gag, and the thought of sharing a bed with one sent negative shivers through his body.

"And you sure you're okay?"

He met his father's gaze again. "Yes, I'm sure, but I'd like to ask you something."

"What?"

"That time when you and Mom were dating and you let her run off to Paris and almost lost her. Why did you do that?"

Over the years Jonas and his brothers had heard the

story of their parents' tumultuous love affair. They'd heard how Drew had refused to accept Eden as his fate and ended up pushing her away. By the time he'd come to his senses, she had left the States for Paris. Drew had freaked out at the possibility of losing Eden forever and had followed her and asked her to marry him.

His father met his gaze for a long moment and then said, "Because I was convinced I was not ready to love her or any woman. I honestly assumed I was above falling in love. I loved women too much to settle down with just one."

Jonas nodded. That pretty much sounded like the story of his life. "What made you see things differently?"

"I asked myself what I thought would be a simple question. Would my life be better without Eden in it? Was chasing women more important than making memories of waking up to the same woman, one who could connect to me on all levels? One who made me think about her when I should be working? One who made me think of having several little girls who would look just like her, even when I thought I didn't even want kids? When I finally was honest with myself and answered those questions, then I knew that whether I wanted to be or not, I was in love. And then I knew there *was* no way I could let her go."

Drew released a chuckle from deep within his chest. "Hell, I had it so bad for her and didn't even know it. I was pure whipped." He paused a moment, then threw in an extra piece of sage advice. "I believe a smart man not only recognizes when he's whipped but actually loves the thought of it, especially if the woman is worth it. There's nothing wrong with falling in love if it's a woman you can't live your life without."

Drew then glanced across the room at his wife, who was sitting down on the sofa talking to their daughters-in-law. "And for me, your mother is that woman. She always will be."

He then met Jonas's gaze again. "So if you're ever lucky to meet such a woman, whatever you do, please don't make the mistake your old man almost made."

Drew smiled then. "Come on. Your mom is beckoning us to dinner."

Jonas drowned out the conversation around him at the dinner table as he ate his food. Everyone seemed to be in a festive mood, so why wasn't he? Fulton had called today to congratulate him on an outstanding marketing campaign. Already voyages on the *Velocity* had sold out for the next six months and they were working on a waiting list that extended well into the next three.

However, what had really consumed Jonas's thoughts for the past three weeks hadn't been the success of *Velocity*'s marketing campaign. It had been Nikki. His Nikki. The woman who'd enticed him to push for a private arrangement with her for two weeks. It was an arrangement he still had memories about today. Never had a woman been so loving, so giving, so downright sexy.

Even now he could recall them dancing together in a nightclub in Sydney, him finally being talked into going shopping with her in Dubai, and the two of them viewing the Eiffel Tower in Paris. Their time together had been so ideal, so perfect. Exactly how it should feel for a couple who cared about each other.

Who had pretended to.

There were times when he was alone in his bed, at work or just riding in his car when he would remember and wish there was a way he could recapture those moments, a way he could book another flight on the *Velocity* and relive every single second. But he knew there was no way he could do that. So all he had was memories.

He felt an ache in the lower part of his gut just remembering all those sexy outfits she'd purchased on her shopping spree and how she would give him a personal fashion show, which ended with him removing every single item, stitch by stitch. Then they would make love all through the night and the early-morning hours.

Jonas glanced up when Tyson asked him a question about the *Velocity*. Moments later Eli and Galen asked him a few more questions. He knew his brothers had noted he was quieter than usual and were trying to draw him into the family's conversation. He appreciated their efforts, but he truly wasn't in a talkative mood tonight.

"So, Jonas, what happens if you get another big account like Fulton's and need a photographer?" Mercury asked.

Jonas frowned, wondering where the hell that question came from and why Mercury was asking. He glanced across the dinner table at his brother. "I'll do like I've always done and use a freelancer. Of course I'll approach Nikki Cartwright first. She's the best." Jonas then quietly returned to his meal.

"Yeah, but that won't be possible now that she's moving to L.A."

Jonas's head snapped back up and his green eyes slammed into his brother's. "What did you just say?" His tone had such a deadly and hard edge to it that everyone at the dinner table stopped eating and stared at him.

Mercury pretended not to notice Jonas's steely disposition when he answered with an insolent smile on his lips. "I said Nikki is moving to L.A. She got this job offer from some big-time producer and I understand she's moving away at the end of the month."

Jonas shifted his gaze from Mercury to Brittany, who was sitting at Galen's side. "Is that true?"

She nodded slowly. "Yes. I thought you knew."

Jonas drew in a deep breath. No, he hadn't known. For some reason he looked at his father, and when their eyes met, Jonas clearly remembered the conversation they'd shared before dinner.

He pushed his plate back and stood. "Please excuse me. I need to leave. There's some business I need to tend to."

Eden, who was completed dumbfounded, spoke up. "Surely whatever it is can wait, Jonas. You haven't finished dinner."

He shook his head. "No, Mom, it can't wait."

And then he headed for the door, only pausing to grab his motorcycle helmet off a table in the foyer on his way out.

Nikki couldn't sleep, but then that was the story of her life since she returned home. Too bad she couldn't get thoughts of Jonas out of her mind. She wondered if he ever thought about her with the same yearning and intensity that she thought about him. Probably not. The only good thing was that his name hadn't been linked with any woman in the tabloids since they'd gotten back, but she knew it was just a matter of time.

She thought about her move to L.A. Of course her parents and brother who lived in San Diego were happy with her decision, since that meant she would be closer to them. She hadn't lived in California since leaving home for college so perhaps the move would do her some good.

And then maybe she would be able to forge ahead with her life and forget about Jonas. Then she wouldn't have to worry about the possibility of running into him unexpectedly or worry whether he was with another woman. Not that it mattered, really. Just remembering all they'd shared was enough to shatter her these days.

And then there was another problem she'd encountered because of Jonas. Her body was going through sexual withdrawal. This time of night when she couldn't sleep, she would remember everything they'd shared, especially the time she'd spent in his arms, making love with him, using all those positions. And during those last fourteen days they *had* made love. She wondered if he'd been able to tell the difference. Probably not.

After a few more tosses and turns she finally sat up in bed. She clicked on a lamp and looked around. For the first time since she moved here she realized just how lonely this house was. Lonely and empty. Her bedroom was prettily decorated in her favorite colors of chocolate and lime green, and she'd hired a professional decorator to make sure things were just how she'd wanted them. But something was missing.

It really didn't matter now since she was moving away. Already her realtor had found a buyer so there was nothing or no one to hold her to Phoenix any longer. She would miss Brittany and their weekly lunch dates, but like she'd told her best friend, they were just an airplane flight away.

Galen had promised to call her the minute Brittany went into labor. More than anything she wanted to be around when her goddaughter or godson was born.

Since it seemed like sleep was out of the question for her at the moment, she slid out of bed and slipped into the matching robe to the baby-doll nightgown she was wearing. Both had been items she'd purchased while in Paris.

She had made it downstairs when she heard the sound of a motorcycle. One of her neighbors had recently purchased a Harley and she figured he'd taken it out for a late-night ride.

Nikki was headed for her kitchen to raid her snack jar. Thanks to Jonas she liked Tootsie Pops and always kept a bag on hand. Whenever she plopped one in her mouth she thought of him.

She stopped walking when she heard a knock on her door. Who on earth would be visiting her at this hour? She tightened her robe around her and went to the door, pausing to take a look out the peephole. Her breath caught in her throat when she saw her late-night caller.

She quickly entered the code to disarm her alarm system before opening the door. "Jonas? Why... What are you doing here?"

He was standing under her porch light in a pair of jeans, a T-shirt that advertised Ideas of Steele, and biker boots. In his hand he held his bike helmet. "Would it be okay if I come inside so we can talk?"

Although she had no idea what they had to talk about, she nodded and took a step back. "Sure. Come in."

Once he entered and closed the door behind him, she watched as he glanced around and saw the boxes already packed and sealed, ready to be picked up by the movers.

"I heard tonight that you're leaving town. I didn't know," he said.

She nodded. So he didn't know. Would it have mattered if he had? She doubted it. "Yes, I got a job offer in L.A."

"Why didn't you tell me you were moving away, Nikki?"

His question surprised her. Why would she tell him? It's not like they meant anything to each other. Those two weeks on board the *Velocity* had been nothing but a game of pretend that he'd initiated under the disguise of a private arrangement. She'd gone along with it because she loved him. And she had no regrets.

"Nikki?"

She met his gaze, suddenly feeling angry when she recalled how he'd started withdrawing from her the last day of their trip. They'd made love true enough, but she'd felt he was pulling back in ways he hadn't before. Now she placed her hands on her hips and lifted her chin to glare at him.

"I really didn't think you'd want to know, Jonas. We had an agreement and you made sure I understood the terms. I did. When we returned to Phoenix, things would go back to the way they were between us. So excuse me, but did I miss something?"

He blew out a long breath and rubbed his hand

across his face; then he looked back at her. "Yes, you missed something, and so did I."

She lifted a brow. "Really? Then please enlighten me because I have no idea what *we* could have missed."

"The fact that I have fallen in love with you."

His words took the wind out of Nikki's sail. She sucked in a deep breath, and it seemed that every muscle in her body tensed. She stared at him, saw his unreadable green eyes staring back at her. She slowly shook her head. "Impossible. You don't know how to love."

"I do now. You taught me, remember? For two weeks you taught me there's a difference between having sex with a woman and making love to one. I know that difference now, Nikki. I've always made love to you because I've always loved you. Since our first kiss, and possibly before it. But I fought it tooth and nail."

He paused a moment and then said in a low voice, "I probably would still be fighting it if I hadn't heard you were leaving. Once I heard I knew I couldn't let you go without telling you how much you mean to me. Just how much I love you."

Nikki closed her eyes, fearful when she opened them he would be gone and his presence would have been only a figment of her imagination. Evidently he'd read her mind, because when she opened her eyes, he said, "I'm still here."

Yes, he was still there, standing in the middle of her living room with his helmet clutched to his hand, his feet braced apart and his hair tied back in a ponytail. He looked like a rebel, a rogue, a man determined to defy the odds. A man who'd managed to claim her heart.

"Why do you love me, Jonas?" she asked, wondering if he really knew or if he only assumed he was in love with her.

"Why *don't* I love you?" he countered. "But to answer your question, I love everything about you. But I especially like how you handle your business. I admire that. And I love the way you make me feel when I'm inside of you, lying beside you in bed, or sitting across from you at a table. I think I fell in love with you that day we met at my office and you came in from the rain. I was so totally captivated by you then, but I tried denying it. And then that day we kissed in your office, I was so taken aback I couldn't think straight. That's why I tried avoiding you for eighteen months. You pulled out emotions in me that I wasn't use to feeling, and I was afraid that you would encompass my whole world. In fact, you do. My only question is how do you feel about me?"

She drew in a deep breath, fighting back tears and thinking only a man like Jonas would have to ask. Anyone else would have been able to see it on her face. "I love you, too, Jonas. I think I fell in love with you that rainy day as well, but I knew for certain how I felt while on the *Velocity*. But I thought loving you was a hopeless case on my part, although I wanted to use those two weeks to show you what love was about."

"You did, sweetheart. I know the difference between sex and making love. Each and every time I touched you, we made love."

"Oh, Jonas."

He placed his helmet on the table and then slowly crossed the room and pulled her into his arms. "Just so you know, me loving you is not about making any demands. More than anything I want you to follow your dream. Move to L.A. if you have to, but I'll be coming with you. I can set up a satellite office and work from just about anywhere."

Nikki's eyes lit up. "You would do that for me?"

"I would do that for *us*. I don't want to be away from you. I got used to having you around on the *Velocity*, and I've been miserable these past three weeks without you."

He paused a moment and then said, "And I need to be completely honest about something, confess to something I did just to keep you around me."

She lifted a brow. "What?"

He reached out, captured her finger and wrapped his bigger one around it. "That night you turned down my job offer I took measures into my own hands."

"How?"

"By playing a favor card. I called a guy I knew whose brother is closely tied with Senator Joseph's election campaign. I had him renege on your job offer."

She stiffened in his embrace. "You did?"

"Yes. I did."

She didn't say anything for a minute, just stared at him. The multitude of emotions revealed in his eyes nearly took her breath away. Even then he had wanted her and had even been willing to play dirty to get her. But she would have to admit that the end result had been worth it.

"I hope you know doing something like that is going to cost you," she said, making sure he heard the lightness in her voice when she began seeing a wary look in his gaze.

"Hmm, what's the charge?"

She paused as if thinking about it and then said,

"You're going to have to love me for the rest of your days."

He drew her closer. "Baby, I had planned on doing that anyway."

And then Jonas lowered his mouth to hers, kissing Nikki with the hunger he had only for her and no other woman. Only with her did he want to feel free, be loved and give love. Only with her did his emotions rise to the top. And only with Nikki was he not afraid to want more than what he'd been getting. He wanted commitment. He wanted to abolish his one-and-done policy and replace it with one-and-only, because that's what Nikki was to him.

He broke off the kiss and swept her off her feet and into his arms. "I need to make love to you. And just so you know, I haven't touched another woman since you. I couldn't because they weren't you and I didn't want anyone else."

He leaned down and kissed her again. When he released her lips, he asked, "Let's go to the bedroom?"

He slowly carried her there, kissing her intermittently along the way. When he reached her bedroom he placed her down in the middle of her bed. He glanced around. "Nice room."

She looked him up and down and smiled. "Mmm, nice man."

He chuckled and likewise, let his gaze travel all over her. "Nice woman."

And then he began removing his clothes, and she watched as he removed every single piece. He then moved back to the bed and with a couple flicks of his wrists, he had removed the robe and gown from her body.

"You're pretty good at that, aren't you?" she said when he'd gotten her naked.

"Only for you, sweetheart," he said against her throat before trailing a path with his tongue past her ear. "And there is something else I'd like to ask you."

"What?" She was barely able to get the word out before his hand lowered between her legs and he quickly moved to the honeyed warmth he knew awaited him there.

"Will you marry me?"

It seemed she had stopped breathing, and he leaned back and stared into her face. She returned his stare and he knew what she was doing. She had to see the sincerity of his question in his features, in his eyes, in the lips he then eased into an earnest smile.

He saw the single tear that fell from her eye before she smiled and said, "Yes, yes. I'll marry you. I'd almost given up hope that I would find him."

He lifted a brow. "Find who?"

"My knight in shining armor." She chuckled. "Little did I know he would be riding a motorcycle instead of a horse, but I'll take him any way I can. My Mr. Wrong became my Mr. Right. I love you so much."

"And I love you, too."

And then he was kissing her again, pulling her into his arms while their limbs entwined. And then he eased over her, slid between her legs, lifted her hips and stared down at her while he penetrated her. He'd never tire of looking down at her while they made love.

"Damn, I miss this. Damn, how I miss you," he said in between deep, languid thrusts. He didn't intend to rush. Instead he made love to her with the patience of a man who had all day and all night. He wondered if she noticed the difference in their lovemaking and figured eventually she would. She wrapped her legs around him and, lifting her hips off the bed, met his thrusts, stroke for stroke.

"Oh Jonas, I miss this, too," she said, as her inner muscles clenched him hard, trying to pull everything out of him.

He threw his head back and screamed her name at the same moment she screamed his. He gripped her hips tightly, needing as much of a connection with her as he could get.

And that's when he knew she felt him, felt him in a way no other woman had felt him before. He was exploding inside of her, christening her insides with his release.

Her shocked eyes looked up at him with delight when she realized he hadn't put on a condom. He didn't intend to use one ever again. This was the woman he would marry, and he wanted babies with her. No other man who would be her babies' daddy. With her he would share everything.

Moments later, when they were both spent, he slumped down in the bed and gathered her into his arms. They would sleep, wake up and make love, sleep and then make love some more. Later. Tomorrow. They would talk and lay out a strategic plan to tackle how they would make things work with her new job in L.A. They were and always would be a team.

"You forced me to realize I wanted the very things I thought I would never desire, Nikki," he whispered, emotions clogging his voice. "But I can see so clearly now and I know what I want, sweetheart. More than anything I want you."

And then he leaned down and slanted his mouth over hers, knowing this was the beginning, and for them there would never be an end.

Epilogue

A beautiful day in June

Nikki glanced around the ballroom that was filled with over five hundred guests who'd come to witness one of Phoenix's most notorious bachelors tying the knot. It had been the kind of wedding she'd always dreamed of having, with her mother and her mother-in-law working together. Her dream had come true.

She glanced across the room at her husband, who was talking to his father and some of his cousins. There were a lot of Steeles, more than she'd known existed, and now she was a part of the family. She and Jonas had decided to alternate living in L.A. and Phoenix. His idea for a satellite office had been a good one.

"You're such a beautiful bride," one of Jonas's female cousins, Cheyenne, the mother of triplets, told her, pulling her back into the conversation. They were standing there talking with Brittany and two more of Jonas's female cousins from Charlotte. Brittany was showing already, and she and Galen had found out a few months ago they would be having twins. Everyone in the Steele family was excited at the thought of multiple births again.

"Thanks." And she felt beautiful, because of Jonas. When she had walked down the aisle to him at the church, it was as if the two of them were the only ones there. The gaze that had held hers spoke volumes and had sent out several silent messages, ones that only she could decipher. That was a good thing. If anyone else had read his thoughts, they would have been scandalized.

"Ladies, I need to borrow my wife for a minute."

She glanced up when Jonas suddenly appeared by her side, sliding his hand into hers. He looked devastatingly handsome dressed in his white tux with his wavy hair flowing about his shoulders. His green eyes were sharp when he glanced down at her. "We'll be leaving in a few minutes and I thought we should say goodbye to our parents before we took off."

She beamed up at him. "Okay."

As a wedding gift, Mr. Fulton had given them the honeymoon suite on board the *Velocity*. They would remain in Dubai for two weeks and would return to the States on the *Velocity* when the airship came back through, making its rounds.

Halfway over to where their parents stood, Jonas stopped and pulled her into his arms and kissed her. She ignored the catcalls and whistles as she sank closer into her husband's embrace. When he finally released her, she smiled up at him. "And what was that for?"

He grinned. "I thought it was time for me to make another public claim. You're mine and I want the whole world to know it."

Nikki was filled with intense happiness. Her head and her heart were no longer at battle. Now they were on the same page, reading from the same script and the writing said *Jonas loves Nikki. Nikki loves Jonas. And they will live happily ever after.*

* * * * *

Two classic Westmoreland novels from
NEW YORK TIMES AND *USA TODAY*
BESTSELLING AUTHOR

BRENDA JACKSON

PROMISES OF SEDUCTION

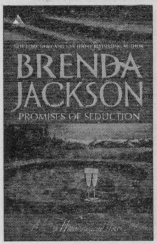

In *The Durango Affair*, one unforgettable night with Savannah Claiborne has turned into a lifetime obligation for bachelor Durango Westmoreland. But his proposal has one condition...that it be a marriage in name only.

In *Ian's Ultimate Gamble*, Ian Westmoreland is shocked to see Brooke Chamberlain at his resort. No woman has come close to igniting his passion as she once did. The stakes are very high... but will Ian's wager pay off?

"Sexy and sizzling." —*Library Journal* on *Intimate Seduction*

On sale now wherever books are sold!

KIMANI PRESS™
www.kimanipress.com

KPBJ4700112

Have you discovered the Westmoreland family?

NEW YORK TIMES AND *USA TODAY*
BESTSELLING AUTHOR

BRENDA JACKSON

Pick up these classic Westmoreland novels...

On Sale Now!

Contains:
Stone Cold Surrender
and *Riding the Storm*

On Sale Now!

Contains:
Jared's Counterfeit Fiancée
and *The Chase Is On*

ARABESQUE®

www.kimanipress.com

KPBJW11SPR

Have you discovered the Westmoreland family?

NEW YORK TIMES AND *USA TODAY*
BESTSELLING AUTHOR

BRENDA JACKSON

**Find out where it all started
with these fabulous 2-in-1 novels.**

On Sale Now!

Contains
Delaney's Desert Sheikh and
Seduced by a Stranger (brand-new)

On Sale Now!

Contains
A Little Dare and
Thorn's Challenge

ARABESQUE®

www.kimanipress.com

KPBJW10SPR

NEW YORK TIMES AND USA TODAY
BESTSELLING AUTHOR

BRENDA JACKSON

A SILKEN THREAD

Masterfully told and laced with the sensuality and drama that Brenda Jackson does best, this is an unforgettable story of relationships at their most complex....

Deeply in love and engaged to be married, Brian Lawson and Erica Sanders can't wait to start their life together. But their perfect world is shattered when a family betrayal causes Erica to leave both town and Brian. Yet when a crisis reunites them years later, neither can deny the passion they still feel for each other. Will Erica and Brian fight to save a love that hangs by a silken thread?

On sale now wherever books are sold!

KIMANI PRESS™
www.kimanipress.com

KPBJASTSPR

A brand-new Madaris novel from

NEW YORK TIMES AND USA TODAY
BESTSELLING AUTHOR

BRENDA JACKSON

INSEPARABLE

A Madaris Family Novel

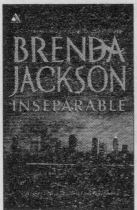

Ever since his cousin Blade got married, Reese has become Houston's most eligible bachelor. He turns to his temporary roommate and best friend, Kenna, for dating advice, and suddenly Reese sees her for the beautiful woman that she is. Even though Kenna's afraid to give her heart to the man who could so easily break it, Reese embarks on a mission of seduction. And when Kenna's life is in jeopardy, she'll discover just how far a Madaris man will go for the woman he loves....

AVAILABLE NOW WHEREVER BOOKS ARE SOLD.

KIMANI PRESS™
www.kimanipress.com

KPBJINSPSPR

NEW YORK TIMES AND USA TODAY
BESTSELLING AUTHOR

BRENDA JACKSON

Look for these Madaris Family novels

TONIGHT AND FOREVER
WHISPERED PROMISES
ETERNALLY YOURS
ONE SPECIAL MOMENT
FIRE AND DESIRE
SECRET LOVE
TRUE LOVE
SURRENDER
SENSUAL CONFESSIONS

Available wherever books are sold.

KIMANI PRESS™
www.KimaniPress.com

KPBJMBL